JERICHO RIDE

Betty Gaard

Greenville, South Carolina

Library of Congress Cataloging-in-Publication Data

Gaard, Betty, 1946-
  Jericho ride / by Betty Gaard
    p. cm.
Summary: While working as a riding instructor at a Texas
church camp over the summer, a teenaged boy decides to repent his sins and commit his life to Jesus Christ.
  ISBN 1-57924-968-X (pbk. : alk. paper)
  [1. Church camps—Fiction. 2. Camps—Fiction. 3. Horse-
manship—Fiction. 4. Christian life—Fiction. 5. Texas—Fiction.] I. Title.
  PZ7.G1112Je 2003
  [Fic]—dc21

                                                      2003008275

Design by Micah Ellis
Composition by Melissa Matos

© 2003 Bob Jones University Press
Greenville, SC 29614

ISBN 1-57924-968-X

15   14   13   12   11   10   9   8   7   6   5   4   3   2   1

To Mama,
You taught me to love God.

CONTENTS

CHAPTER

1

A little past midnight, over six hours behind schedule, the bus pulled to a stop on the outskirts of Del Rio. I gathered my gear, dodging the feet and elbows of sleeping passengers. The driver pulled the door open, and a whoosh of warm, dry air filled the front of the bus. I hesitated on the last step. The town was dark—locked up for the night. Even the bus station was closed with only the glow of the drink machine to identify the front door.

"Get off or sit back down," the driver said.

I stepped down, and the bus moved out before the door slammed shut. A fog of diesel fumes settled over me.

"This is a mistake," I said aloud to myself. I was alone in a state I had never set foot in before the bus crossed the border hours earlier. "Come on, Uncle Jack," I said, looking up and down the street. I took a firm grip on my two canvas bags and moved them to a bench along the dark wall outside the bus station. Then I eased down on the bench and tried to relax. *So what do I do now?*

When I heard the rumble of a struggling engine heading my way, I stood and took the straps of my bags in my sweaty palms, prepared to meet my uncle for the first time. But the pickup rounded the corner, moved slowly into sight, and then passed the bus station without pausing. I sank back down on the bench.

"Changed my mind, Mom. I don't want to go," I said, thinking of my computer and all the comforts of home. To the east, faint shadows outlined stores and other businesses. A dim security glow came from dingy windows in the hardware store. To the west, an elementary school lay almost hidden in the shadows of leafy sycamore trees. A single yellow bulb, discouraging mosquitoes and other flying insects, cast a pale glow across the front of the building. A diner stood near the school, with a neon sign boasting the best hamburgers in Texas—open twenty-four hours. It was as silent and dark as the rest of the town.

I shoved my larger bag to the ground, swung my feet up on the bench, took off my baseball cap, and eased my head down on my other bag.

I searched the dark sky, surprised to see stars in the blackness. No moon, but hundreds of stars. Slowly the silence around me seemed to come alive. The soft hum of the drink machine caught my attention. A cricket in the tall weeds made a chirping sound, and then hundreds of crickets chirped. Half a block away a bullfrog croaked, and others answered. A mosquito buzzed near my ear, and I slapped at the side of my face.

"Nice welcome," I mumbled. "So much for Texas-size hospitality." After two years, Oklahoma City seemed like home. For my first twelve years, Wisconsin had been home, and the transition to Oklahoma had been rough, especially after the accident.

Just don't think about it, I told myself for the thousandth time.

Something brought me to my feet. *Is someone out there?* I leaned forward and strained into the darkness past the diner. The orange glow of a cigarette pierced the darkness. Deliberately, I stood tall and forced myself to breathe deeply. I waited as the form of a man walked closer.

"Vincent?"

"Tony Vincent. Yes, sir."

"Let's go."

I grabbed my gear and hurried to follow the stranger. I matched his stride. "Uncle Jack?"

"Ruben."

He was parked just past the diner in the shadows of a coyotillo tree. I tossed my bags into the back of the pickup and climbed into the cab as it left the curb in second gear. The passenger door flew open in the breeze, and I caught the edge of the open window and pulled the door shut. I scowled and thought again, *This is definitely a mistake.* The darkness made it hard to size up Ruben, but he was small, dark-skinned, and even his large straw hat didn't hide his stringy hair. We rode in silence for more than half an hour, and I dozed off and on. I refused to allow myself to think about tomorrow, and the tomorrows of the rest of the summer. A road sign flashed by at an intersection. San Antonio, 165 miles.

"Camp's just ahead." They were the first words Ruben had spoken since the bus station.

I straightened and stared at the trees and dense brush as the pickup turned north off the pavement and onto a narrow gravel road. The headlights flashed across a weathered, hand-painted sign that read *Jericho Road.*

The pickup slowed to a crawl and then stopped almost completely to ease over the deepest ruts. It bounced over smaller holes and rocks. Tree branches slapped at the open window and forced me to lean back and away from the stinging switches. I flinched at every near miss. Mile after mile of gravel ruts and overhanging tree branches convinced me that the isolation I was headed for would be a high price for the prize I had dreamed of for two years. *But this prize is worth any price,* I thought.

"How much farther?" I had tried not to ask.

"Gone five. Four to go." Ruben was a man of few words.

Nine miles off the paved road. Incredible. How will I ever get back to the bus station!

We rocked and bounced over the next four miles in a tense twenty-five minutes, and then we were suddenly in a clearing. The sky was dark, with only a faint trail of light smoke from a campfire a mile or so in the distance. A crudely carved sign stood attached to a tall post. "Welcome to Camp Jericho." The clearing stretched on and on, and the truck picked up speed on the packed and graded road. Its head-lights skimmed the west side of a large open-sided pavilion that covered rows of picnic tables. About three hundred feet past the pavilion was a larger building that looked like it was made of rock. I glanced over at Ruben, expecting some kind of information about the camp or these buildings. But Ruben was no tour guide.

About a quarter mile past the rock building, he slowed the pickup and made a right turn back onto dirt and gravel. *The stable,* I thought. The strong smell of fresh hay and horses brought a sense of home and a purpose for being here. The familiar smell was comforting. I sighed, thinking of Guardian and the other horses back home.

The truck came to a stop in front of a small wooden cabin that could have passed for an abandoned hunting shack. A bare light bulb lit the planked front porch and had also at-tracted what looked like half of the flying insects in south-west Texas.

"You'll bunk in there," Ruben said, and then gave a slight nod of his head in the direction of the cabin. A gold-capped tooth flashed in the light as he spoke. "Showers over there." He turned slightly and gestured toward a shed about fifty feet across from the bunkhouse.

I opened the door of the pickup and hesitated as my right shoe hung above the ground. Then I remembered the bus driver's impatience and stepped out quickly and took both bags from the bed of the truck. "Thanks."

I stood without moving for several moments and watched the taillights of the pickup move down the road until it turned out of sight just past the stable. I moved my larger bag to the porch and then picked up the smaller one and walked toward the dark shed. *I've gotta be overripe from almost two days on that bus,* I thought.

I searched in the darkness of the shed and found a pull string that turned on the light and dimly lit the shower and bathroom area. The quick, cold shower felt good and washed away some of the stiffness of the long hours on the bus. When I saw no hooks and no other towels, I stuffed my damp towel into a plastic sack, and the sack into my canvas bag.

The wide, rough planks of the porch creaked as I entered the bunkhouse with both bags. I latched the screen door and waited for my eyes to adjust to the darkness. The small cabin held a chest of drawers and three sets of bunk beds. Five pairs of boots stood here and there around the room. *Smells like leather and sweaty socks in here,* I thought.

I moved the only chair in the room near the head of the only available bed, then slipped off my gym shoes, climbed up on the top bunk, and as quietly as possible, eased my tired body onto the full length of the bare mattress. I gradually became aware of the soft sounds of snoring all around me. Within moments, the sounds seemed to swell and fill the room. After a while, I could sort out individual snores and predict sighs and snorts. Then a high-pitched buzz in my ear let me know that I hadn't made it through the door fast enough. I slapped at the mosquito and wished I had a sheet to pull up over my head.

Moments later a sound like a scream far in the distance jolted my nerves and set my heart racing. Seconds later I heard more screaming. I sat up, my head just inches from the ceiling, and looked at the bunks across from me. No one stirred. I waited and listened to the sounds rise and fall. Silence settled for several moments, and then the screaming came again.

I shuddered and squeezed my eyes shut. *One summer at this camp and probation will end. I'll qualify for the scholarship. I can handle it. I've just got to handle it.* Eventually I slept.

The morning sun caught my closed eyes. I stretched and squeezed my eyes more tightly shut, momentarily disoriented. Seconds later my mind cleared. I sat up, flung my feet and legs off the side of the high bunk, and slid to the floor with a thud. I stood alone in the small room. The boots that had cluttered the floor hours earlier were gone, and the chair that had served as a ladder to my bunk was standing by the door. A stack of clean towels, folded bed linens, and a pillow lay on the chair.

"Thanks." I guess those were meant for me. I picked up my small bag and headed for the shed. In the morning light it was easy to see that the flimsy branches of several small coyotillo trees served as "hooks" for the guys' wet towels. I dug mine from my bag and tossed it over a low branch.

Several minutes later I made my way through dense brush and scraggly bush-high trees, following a narrow trail that led in the general direction of the open-sided pavilion. The rows of picnic tables had suggested food. My stomach suggested breakfast.

The sound of humming and the clang of pots and pans brought the first signs of life in the camp. I followed the sounds around to the open side of the pavilion, uneasy about the welcome—or lack of one—that I might get.

"Ahh, there you are." A large, smiling lady hurried over as she wiped soapsuds on a stained apron. "Been keeping your breakfast hot." She stepped up real close and gave me a pat on the back. "I'm Frances." She paused to look me over. "Come. Sit."

I winced a little at her overwhelming closeness and then took a step back and sat astride a bench. "Thanks."

"Coyotes keep you awake last night?"

"Coyotes?" Ahh . . . the screaming sounds.

"They don't usually carry on quite as bad as they did last night." She shrugged and shook her head. "Coffee or milk?" she asked, and then answered her own question. "Milk. Be right back."

Frances lumbered back toward the enclosed end of the pavilion. Her jean skirt fell well below her knees and mostly covered her heavy legs, and her ample feet more than covered her rubber shower thongs. A thick bush of hair surrounded her head like a gray halo. I heard her humming again.

In a quick glance around the building I saw a high-pitched A-frame ceiling with bare rafters covered with sheets of corrugated tin. Enough four-foot fluorescent tubes hung from the ceiling to light up half the camp, and six wobbly ceiling fans guaranteed to blow away the gnats and mosquitoes. I sat looking down the long row of tables with picnic bench seats. Two rows of tables filled the pavilion and could easily seat close to one hundred campers and staff members.

Staff member.

It had a nice ring to it.

"Here you go." Frances set a breakfast tray in front of me, bringing me out of my reverie.

"Thanks." I reached for the tall glass of milk. "Where is everyone?"

"Sunday service."

"Oh." *I haven't been to Sunday school or church since the accident,* I thought.

"No boots?" Frances gestured toward my thistle and briar covered shoes and jeans.

I couldn't help glancing down at her almost bare feet as I momentarily struggled for a response.

"The Professor's been waiting for you," Frances said.

The Professor?

Frances left to fill her coffee cup. The kitchen lay at one end of the long narrow pavilion with large, screenless windows on three sides. Four-by-eight sheets of plywood hung by hinges from the tops of the openings and were propped open with long sticks, forming canopies over the openings.

"Probably no TV out here," I muttered as I reached for my third biscuit.

"You always talk to yourself?"

I spun around on the bench, surprised to face a tall green-eyed girl about my age. "Uh . . . no . . . well, yeah, I guess I do."

"I'm Mary," she said. Her thick, blond hair fell in a braid down her back. A yellow ribbon held the end of the braid, and blue-rimmed sunglasses rested on top of her head.

"I'm Tony."

"I know. The Professor's been waiting for you. We've all been waiting for you."

"Guess I need an alarm clock," I said. I felt my face flush warm.

Mary shrugged. "Nah, you won't need a clock around here. The guys let you sleep in."

A wet touch to the back of my arm brought me up off the bench.

"Meet Sabado," Mary said, stroking the soft shining coat of the golden retriever.

"Sabado. That's Spanish, isn't it?"

"Right—means Saturday."

I dropped to one knee on the wood planked floor and vigorously patted Sabado as I lifted the dog's nose to within inches of my own. "You're a thoroughbred for sure."

Mary leaned over and gave Sabado another pat. "I see you have a weakness for dogs."

"Yeah, dogs and horses. We just understand each other."

"Tony." The deep voice of authority and quiet confidence instantly drew our attention. I straightened. My mouth opened slightly, but no sounds came.

"Uncle Jack," I said, almost in a whisper. I stared at him. My breath stopped. *He looks just like Dad.*

CHAPTER

2

In the two years since the accident, my mind picture of Dad had started to dim, and now here Uncle Jack stood—almost the image of Dad.

He was a big man, a smiling powerful man. His light reddish-brown moustache matched his hair and heavy eyebrows. Even his blotchy red face seemed to match. A small horn from a real bull hung from a leather strap around his neck, and a notebook caused his shirt pocket to bulge.

Mary suddenly seemed aware of the tension as she looked from Uncle Jack to me. "You okay?" she asked.

Her voice brought my mind back to the present, and I took a clumsy step toward Uncle Jack with my hand outstretched. "Hello." The sound of my heartbeat pounded in my ears.

Uncle Jack's arms were beginning to reach out for a hug, but he instantly shifted his position and took my hand in both of his own. His handshake was brisk and affectionate, and lingered longer than necessary.

I clenched my jaw, took a deep breath, and deliberately stepped back.

"I'm sorry I couldn't wait for your bus," Uncle Jack said. "We had an emergency here at camp, and I was called back. I hope Ruben took good care of you."

"Yes, sir."

"Did Ruben talk your ears off?" Mary laughed at her question.

I nodded and couldn't help a quick grin.

"You met the guys in the bunkhouse?"

"No. I haven't met anyone. Well . . . just Mary and Frances."

Uncle Jack hesitated, looking confused. "Jordan didn't greet you and get you settled?"

"Jordan?"

"Jordan. Your cousin." Uncle Jack looked toward the floor and gave a slight shake of his head, then was distracted by my shoes. "No boots?"

"No, sir," I said, and then I lowered my head a little and added softly, "Left 'em on the bus."

Uncle Jack nodded and turned to introduce me to the staff members returning from Sunday service. I noticed immediately that boots were definitely the "in thing" at Camp Jericho! Frances and I were the only nonconformists.

"Meet Tony Vincent," Uncle Jack said.

One by one Uncle Jack pointed to the six young adults and called out their names. The three girls and three guys were all dressed in jeans, and all wore or carried cowboy hats.

"Hey," I said.

"Tony's the best riding instructor in Oklahoma." Uncle Jack radiated pride as he pounded my back with affectionate whacks. "You'll get to know each other in the next few weeks." Uncle Jack looked toward the kitchen and then gave a dismissive wave to the group.

"Jordan." Uncle Jack called to a frowning teenager who stood across the pavilion. "Come meet your cousin."

Jordan moved across the wood planks, and the soles of his boots made soft scraping sounds as they brushed the wood with every step. His light reddish-brown hair hung below the neck of his tee shirt and was almost exactly the same shade as his father's. He stood shorter than me, and a lot shorter than his dad. His heavily blemished face relaxed its frown only slightly.

"So, Tony slipped by you last night," Uncle Jack said, laying a hand on Jordan's sloping shoulder.

"Yeah . . . I guess I went to sleep. Sorry, Dad."

"I was pretty late," I said. "Couldn't expect anyone to wait up that long. No problem. Really." I shifted from foot to foot. *Come on. Let's get this over with,* I thought.

Uncle Jack sat, slung his legs over the bench to face the table, and gestured for Jordan and me to join him. Mary set a cup of coffee in front of Uncle Jack and then sat down next to Jordan. She stroked Sabado.

"We're glad you're here, Tony," Uncle Jack said. "You'll be a big part of an exciting summer for hundreds of kids during the next ten weeks."

I nodded.

"We have about seventy campers every week. Fourth, fifth, and sixth graders. To them, you'll have as much authority as anyone here—and as much responsibility. Maybe more, considering that many of these kids are not experienced on horses."

Uncle Jack's eyes are exactly like Dad's. I fought to keep my emotions in control.

"You'll be the camp's head riding instructor. Jordan will drag the trail and make himself available as you need him."

I was aware of Jordan's slumped shoulders and downcast eyes. His emotions seemed to be silently revolting against the position his dad was putting him in.

"Well, Jordan," Uncle Jack said, "how about bringing up Quarto and Frenchie while I catch up a little with Tony."

Jordan stiffened slightly. "Quarto?"

Uncle Jack nodded in Jordan's general direction. "Quarto is his mother's horse," he said, "but Lisa seldom rides."

Jordan shuffled away from the pavilion in the direction of the stable, and Mary and Sabado joined Frances in the kitchen.

"You'll like Quarto. He has an IQ higher than—" Uncle Jack laughed, but didn't finish his sentence.

He suddenly seemed awkward, and his voice got husky and sort of raspy. He stroked his moustache with two fingers. "I'm really sorry about your dad, Tony."

I took a deep, slow breath and braced myself against the waves of emotion that always threatened to erupt. *Don't think about it. Just don't think about it.*

"I'd have been there for you if I'd known. I guess your mom told you we were out of the country."

I nodded, hoping the heart-to-heart would end quickly.

"But of course God was there for you," he said.

God was there for me?

"We were doing mission work in Mexico for several months before I got the news . . . and then . . . well . . ." Uncle Jack's voice trailed off, and his big hands gestured helplessly above the rough wood table.

"Your mother told me about your trouble at school. Fighting, right?"

"Yes, sir. Lots of fights. Over anything. Over nothing."

"Umm. And now probation," Uncle Jack said.

I nodded. "A successful summer here, and the probation is over."

"Well, God sent you here to help you in this time of trouble."

God sent me here? I wasn't so sure.

The sound of Jordan and the two horses brought a welcome end to the conversation.

"Show Tony around," Uncle Jack said to Jordan.

Quarto, a light-brown bay with black mane and black lower legs, stood calmly waiting. I patted his muzzle and spoke softly to him for several minutes while Jordan stared off in the distance. I thought of Guardian and sighed. That deep reddish-brown stallion had been a constant companion for two years. It had been hard to leave him.

I mounted Quarto slowly and felt good about the response I got from the horse. A little sullen, Jordan turned Frenchie, a golden chestnut flecked with white, in the direction of the large rock building and moved toward it without enthusiasm.

"We have Sunday services in there." Jordan was riding away from the rock building before I could respond. "Out this way," Jordan waved generally to the west, "are the girls' cabins. They're strictly off-limits to the guys, including us, when we have campers."

I looked, but didn't see the cabins.

"Boys' cabins are down that trail." Jordan pointed toward the east but headed north. "Frances and Mary live up this road." Jordan left the wide road and took a narrow trail, allowing Frenchie to pick his way through brush and cactus. Quarto followed, and I drew my knees up a little to avoid the stinging brush and small tree limbs. We rode about twenty minutes and then stood at the edge of a deep canyon. "Devil's River," Jordan said, looking down into the canyon below.

Then he turned Frenchie toward the stable. I followed, but I'd learned only that there were both boys' and girls' cabins, that Frances had a home on the property, and that Devil's River was beautiful. I assumed I'd learn the ropes on a need-to-know basis.

I returned Quarto to the stable and then limped back to the pavilion where I sat alone using my pocketknife to dig cactus and briars from my gym shoes. "Ten weeks, just ten weeks," I said quietly to myself.

"There you go again."

I looked up into Mary's friendly eyes and felt my face flush warm again.

"That was a quick tour."

I shrugged and then winced as I pulled a thorn from my shoe. This one made it all the way through.

"Tell you what. After lunch I'll show you around myself and give you some history. Come help me with lunch setup."

"Uh . . . I'm not much help around the kitchen."

"You will be," Mary said without looking back.

Before I could put away my pocketknife, Uncle Jack startled me.

"Didn't take you long to tour the place," he said. Then he held out a well-worn pair of Justins. "Try these." He handed over the dark leather boots.

"Thanks," I mumbled, completely failing to express the pleasure I felt at the sight of the boots. I gripped them like a treasure. "Thanks," I said again. This time my eyes found Uncle Jack's, and he smiled.

I carefully eased the shoes off my bruised feet and easily pulled the boots on. Then I stood—two inches taller than before.

"Well," Uncle Jack said, "wear a couple pair of socks to fill in. And," he rubbed his moustache and stared thoughtfully at a wobbly fan, "I think we have an extra hat around somewhere."

I took long, heavy strides across the pavilion and joined the small kitchen crew.

Half an hour later, at the sound of the bullhorn, I wiped my hands on my apron and stood ready to serve plates. Staff members seemed to appear from every direction. "How often do we work in the kitchen?" I whispered to Mary.

"As often as we have nothing else to do."

Mary and I sat with Frances, finishing fried chicken and mashed potatoes almost as good as Mom's. The rest of the staff had been served, had eaten, and were back to work. The guys—David, Tyler, and Dudley—were all several years older than me. And the girls—Amy, Rose, and María—were college students.

"Frances is a great cook," Mary said as we watched her trudge toward the kitchen with a stack of dirty dishes. It was Jordan's turn to help clean up.

"Looks like she's enjoyed plenty of her own cooking," I said, and then was immediately sorry I'd said it.

Mary ignored the comment and reached for her hat. "Ready?" Sabado ran a few steps ahead, appearing eager for the tour.

I had to hurry to catch up. "Is Uncle Jack really a professor?"

Mary stopped suddenly. "You sure don't know your uncle very well, do you?"

"I don't know him at all. Haven't seen him since I was a baby. He was my dad's brother, but they were never close."

"Was your dad's brother?" Mary spoke the words cautiously—softly—as if she was unsure of how far to pry.

After a pause, I spoke flatly and without emotion. "Dad was killed in an accident two years ago."

Mary was quiet for a moment. "I'm sorry."

We walked silently to the rock building.

"We call this building the library. Your uncle built it with his own hands and the help of a group of volunteers from the Del Rio churches," Mary said.

"Library?"

"Yeah. Jordan called it a library when he was about four, and, well . . . the name stuck."

Coyotillo trees, with their small greenish flowers, grew densely around the building, partly covering the windows and effectively blending the large rock building into the craggy landscape.

Mary opened the heavy wooden doors, and I followed her inside. The huge room was cool and mostly dark. The ceiling was high—almost two stories—and vaulted with rough beams crisscrossing support. The windows were large and needed washing. A handmade pulpit stood at the front of the room, and row after row of wooden benches with high backs filled the place. I imagined a hundred fourth graders singing "Jesus Loves Me." It sounded good.

"The Professor says when we lose track of God's presence, this is a good place to come to get in touch again."

"Oh." I was at a loss for words.

"Come on," she said, and headed east. From Jordan's short tour, I knew we were walking toward the boys' cabins.

"No horses?" We passed within shouting distance of the stable.

"No need."

We walked in silence, and I watched my boots kick up dust.

"So . . . ," Mary said, "exactly why are you here? I mean, I know you're great with horses, but you're sort of a mystery . . . coming so suddenly."

I smiled at the thought. *A mystery.* "Well . . ." I considered for a moment just how much of myself I really wanted her to know. *Oh, what difference did it make, anyhow?* "I'm one of three applicants hoping for one scholarship to Greenwood Equestrian High School near Oklahoma City. Tuition costs thousands. One scholarship is offered every year, and I'm determined to earn it."

"So-o-o . . . you train horses," Mary ventured.

"Sometimes, but mostly I'll be taught how to teach other people to work with horses."

Mary hesitated, still wondering. "Then . . . you need more experience to get in?"

"I need paid teaching experience. I need this summer for the record. I need something to make my record look better than the other guys." I thought about the probation and then dismissed the thought.

Mary seemed satisfied with the explanation, but I knew she didn't have the faintest clue about the depth of my desire for a successful summer at this camp. Winning that scholarship meant a chance to start making up for Dad's final sacrifice. *I've just got to get in at Greenwood.* My stomach muscles drew up in a tight knot at the thought of failure. *I've got to get in.*

I gestured in the general direction of the stable and hurried to match Mary's stride. "I thought you all would be riding everywhere."

"Nope. And Frances doesn't like the horses near the kitchen. They stir up dust."

Uncle Jack and Jordan had ignored that rule, I thought.

Then, three echoes from the bullhorn filled the air.

"Come now," Mary said, translating.

We reached the pavilion out of breath, but there was no sign of Uncle Jack. Then the bullhorn sounded again.

"That way," Mary said.

After a ten-minute hustle through trails and narrow paths, we stepped out into a clearing not fifty feet from the bunkhouse. It took a few seconds to make sense of the scene before us. Uncle Jack stood near the front porch with several of the camp's staff. Jordan, mounted on Frenchie, waited nearby. The main attraction, though, was two Val Verde County Sheriff's deputy's cars parked up close to the porch. The dust seemed to be settling on the patrol cars as if they had screeched to a stop only moments earlier. Two deputies leaned against the cars, looking casual but in control.

"Tony." Uncle Jack was calling and identifying me in the same tone.

I joined him without taking my eyes off the deputies.

"Tony Vincent?" The huge bulk of the officer stepped up close.

"Yes, sir." I removed my cap and glanced at Uncle Jack.

"Step inside, son," one of the officers said.

I looked at Uncle Jack again before I moved, saw his slight confirming nod, and then went inside the bunkhouse.

Uncle Jack followed, and then the two deputies entered and let the screen door slam shut. The overwhelming presence of the deputies seemed to fill the entire room like a quart in a pint container. Their huge beefy arms were heavily covered with dense hair—one man was much darker than the other—giving them both bearlike appearances.

Where do they find these guys? I thought, bewildered, but not frightened.

"These your bags?" The bear with the name tag reading *Cole* was pointing to my two canvas bags.

I could only nod. It was becoming obvious that trouble filled the room, and I was moving from anxious to frightened. *What did these guys want?*

"Mind emptying the bags, please?" Mr. Polite with the darker arms stood only inches away. His large frame seemed to tower above even Uncle Jack.

I reached up to the top bunk and pulled down the small bag, unzipped it, and began pulling out personal belongings. Within a minute my toothbrush, soap, deodorant, razor for my weekly shave, and a small pile of dirty laundry lay in a humiliating heap on the floor. From my half-crouched position, I looked up into the broad face of Deputy Cole and waited.

The deputy gestured with his chin to the larger bag, and I stood and pulled it down from the bunk, unzipped it, and began pulling out its contents. Outside, most of the staff stood silently, watching through the open door and windows.

I couldn't help remembering how carefully Mom had packed the things I was now lifting from the bag. Two pair of jeans, several tee shirts, a pile of socks, and then . . . and then . . . with my mouth open and my chest pounding, I stared at the bottom of the bag. I was breathing, but it wasn't easy. The shiny metal I stared at was certainly not in the bag when Mom helped pack it.

"Move away from the bag, son." The deputy was stone-faced.

After I stood and took a step back, he took a clean white cloth and reached into the bag and removed a .44 Magnum Smith & Wesson by its barrel. The dark wood grip looked well used and discolored by the sweat and oil of many hands.

I bit my lip and vowed not to let a tear fall. *Big mistake, Mom, big mistake.* Dreams of Greenwood Equestrian High School began to fade. Probation forever. Unless this was cleared up, I had about two chances of getting into the academy: slim and none.

My eyes met Uncle Jack's. I saw Dad's eyes and an overwhelming sense of disappointment—again.

CHAPTER

3

An hour later, I sat with Dudley at the pavilion. Uncle Jack had sent the rest of the staff back to their various activities. Dudley was the camp's summer speaker and one of the boys' cabin counselors. I sat hunched over the table, my fingers tightly intertwined, and the heels of my boots nervously moving up and down over the wood floor. Dudley sat across from me, lightly fingering the brim of his hat, turning it slowly around and around.

"This is a mistake," I said, barely above a whisper. "I don't know anything about that gun."

Dudley nodded. "Try not to worry. The sheriff's department will trace the gun. They'll find the truth."

"Yeah, but what if they don't?" My fear of losing this chance at Greenwood overshadowed everything else. *I've got to get that scholarship. I've just got to.* My chest tightened, and my breathing became shallow and labored.

"Well, let's pray about it," Dudley said, and then without taking a breath, he launched into a long appeal for God's mercy and justice—both for me and for the person responsible for putting the gun in my bag.

When he finished, I was breathing easier, but not much.

"A verse of Scripture comes to mind," Dudley said. "Psalm 46:1 says, 'God is our refuge and strength, a very present help in trouble.' Just remember," he said, "God is here and He's in control. He'll see you through this."

I wasn't so sure.

Moments later, the two patrol cars flew past the pavilion, leaving us in a cloud of dust and with a head full of unanswered questions.

An anonymous phone call had tipped them off, Deputy Cole had said. But who? And why?

Uncle Jack appeared through the bushes, looking solemn and thoughtful. "Tony," he said, straddling the bench, "try not to worry. We'll trust God to see you through this. The Val Verde County Sheriff's Department will do a ballistics check on the gun, and hopefully they'll trace it to the source of all this confusion."

"Well . . ." I glanced at Dudley. "But what if they don't?" *Was this a repeat of the conversation I'd had minutes earlier?*

"They will. We'll just have to trust God." Uncle Jack pulled his journal from his pocket and began to make notes. The small notebook, Mary had said, was a daily record of camp activities and an attempt to stretch and balance camp finances.

Trust God? I thought. *Wasn't it God who let Dad die?*

I only nodded. At least Uncle Jack and Dudley seemed to believe me.

Minutes later, Mary and Sabado walked toward the pavilion. "Ready to finish the tour?"

"Oh . . . yeah, sure," I said, grateful that Mary wasn't asking questions about the mysterious gun. I took a deep breath and tried to shake the heaviness that lingered.

Just past the rock building a black-tailed jackrabbit crossed the path in front of us in two quick jumps. Sabado made a move to lunge after him, but apparently thought better of it and stayed on the path.

"Where are you from?" I asked.

"Right here."

"I mean when camp is over."

"Right here." Mary spread both hands to indicate here. "I've lived here since I was five."

"Wow. What about school?" Surely she doesn't take the nine miles of ruts and dips every morning, and no school bus would try it.

"Home school."

I was thinking about the boredom of sitting in a makeshift classroom when Mary interrupted my thoughts.

"This narrow trail is off-limits to campers. They're allowed only on the wide, cleared paths."

"Oh yeah? Why?"

"Snakes."

Right away my eyes darted intently ahead, examining the trail and the brush bordering it. She was probably kidding, and I struggled not to show a reaction.

"Not really." I had tried not to say it.

"Well, not usually, but . . . yeah, that's why the campers stay on well-traveled paths."

I fell several steps behind her and did my best to stay in the center of the narrow trail, away from the snake-infested brush. I had a vivid imagination.

"Where do Uncle Jack and Jordan live?" I asked, once we were back on the wide path.

Mary looked at me as if my ignorance was astounding. "The Professor and your Aunt Lisa live straight north of the stable about half a mile. During the summer, Jordan stays in the bunkhouse."

"I guess Dudley, David, and Tyler were also in the bunk-house last night?"

"Right. And Mole."

"Mole?"

"You'll meet him later. Half the time he sleeps in the stable."

"That's Devil's River down there," Mary said. She admired the view while I took off my cap and wiped beads of sweat from my face with the crook of my arm. Even the breeze didn't cool things down. I thought of Guardian, my horse back home, and wished for Quarto but tried not to say so.

"The sides of the canyons around here," she gestured widely, "hide dozens—probably hundreds—of caves."

"Caves?" My head jerked up.

"Dozens of them," Mary said, waving generally in the direction of the canyon. "There's also a lot of really old Indian art on the walls of a lot of the caves. Val Verde County has over four hundred archaeological sites."

That sounds like a gross exaggeration, I thought, *but I can't wait to see for myself.*

We took the trail that the horses had traveled earlier and eventually came out near the library and then continued to walk north. One good whiff of the stable broke my resolve to quit mentioning the horses.

"Sure you don't want to ride?" It seemed like an innocent question.

"No! No! I don't want to ride—*ever,*" Mary shouted, as she leaned forward at the waist, her arms rigidly by her side, and her hands forming tight fists. Her green eyes flashed, and her face flushed a raging red for only seconds before she wheeled away, covered her face with her hands, and began to apologize. "I'm sorry, Tony. I'm sorry. I'm so sorry."

Sabado lunged to her side and searched her face.

My boots were suddenly attached to the ground. My hands fluttered helplessly just above her back and shoulders, wanting to comfort, apologize, console, but how? I stood gaping in disbelief, my eyebrows raised an inch and my jaw hanging open. *What did I say?*

Mary sighed and turned back around after hearing my stammering, faltering attempts at words. "Forgive me. I'll explain . . . sometime," she said with a sad smile, wiping her eyes and giving a helpless palms-up gesture.

"Then let's change the subject."

A long, uncomfortable pause hung in the air before Mary spoke. "What kind of work did your dad do?"

I closed my eyes and spoke slowly. "He was a horse trainer."

Mary laughed timidly and wiped her eyes again. "Sorry I asked."

"He was the best. I miss him so much I can't even . . ." I couldn't finish.

"My mom was killed in a riding accident when I was five," Mary said. "That was eight years ago. I can't even re-member her face," she said slowly, shaking her head.

I kicked the deep ruts in the road and tried to sound as compassionate as I felt. "No wonder you don't like horses."

Mary didn't seem to hear as she kept on talking, her eyes unfocused as she, too, kicked the ruts. "I moved out here the same month. Jordan was six. We grew up together."

We walked the rest of the quarter mile in silence.

I heard humming before I saw her. Frances swept the porch and seemed engrossed in faraway thoughts. The small wood frame house looked newly painted with its blue shutters and white walls. Two huge cottonwood trees poured shade over almost the entire home and yard. A battery-powered golf cart sat with a canvas tarpaulin flung partly over it. Dozens of sunflowers stood four feet tall where the shade ended and the sunlight streamed down.

"Hi, Gram," Mary called.

Gram? I jerked my eyes toward Mary to see if she was serious. I thought of the unkind remark I'd made about Frances enjoying too much of her own good cooking, and I felt my face get hot.

"Giving Tony a tour?" Frances said without breaking pace with the broom.

"The deluxe tour," Mary said. She opened the front door and motioned for me to follow. Then she went to the refrigerator and poured us both iced tea.

I stared at her for several moments, thinking and trying to sort out relationships.

"Yes, she's my grandmother," Mary whispered.

After only a few minutes, Mary said, "We'll be back in time to help with supper."

"Kitchen again?"

"As often as we have nothing else to do."

I'm pretty sure I can find something else to do, I thought.

A ten-minute walk along a narrow path, bordered with tall brush and short scraggly trees—and probably a few venomous snakes—ended in a clearing and another home. A larger home, with an attached carport that covered a red Plymouth Voyager. This time Mary knocked on the door before entering and calling loudly, "Aunt Lisa?"

She turned and said quietly, "Everyone calls her Aunt Lisa."

Aunt Lisa stepped out onto the porch. "Tony, my, how you've grown," she said, and then reached up to give me a quick hug.

I shifted from foot to foot for several minutes while Aunt Lisa talked. "We're so glad you're here," she said again.

Then, "Would you like to see the house?"

I felt like I could see the entire house from where I stood, but I nodded.

"The kitchen," she said, pointing to the obvious. "Jordan's room—during the school year." Aunt Lisa shrugged and frowned, as if she had custody of her son only on alternate weekends. "And this is the classroom." She stood pointing, waiting, until I felt obliged to inspect the classroom. I was surprised. Two computers with scanner, printer, and several other peripherals covered a long table on one side of the room. Two standard-size school desks and one large office desk also filled the crowded room.

"Hmmm." I nodded.

"Aunt Lisa writes freelance magazine articles."

"Oh?" *Now that sounded kind of important.*

"When we ever get phone lines out here, we'll have Internet access too," Aunt Lisa said this mostly to herself, as if it were a nagging concern.

"No phones?" I suddenly felt cut off from civilization. Mom would be waiting to hear from me.

"A cell phone, but it's hard to get a connection because of the hills and canyons around here."

Suddenly we heard a loud commotion as Jordan approached the back yard, leaning low on Frenchie as though a squad of wild Indians was on his tail. Frenchie came to a halt just short of plowing through the kitchen door.

"Not today." Jordan tossed the phone to his mom and reached for the refrigerator door. "Total static."

Aunt Lisa sighed and worked up a faint smile. "Last night we had good reception."

CHAPTER

4

An hour later I handed Frances a big bowl filled with washed and peeled potatoes. She gestured with her knife to a pile of carrots, ready to be washed, scraped, and cut into stew-sized pieces.

"Sunday night beef stew won't be the same," Mary complained.

I looked down at my growing pile of sliced carrots and wondered how she could do better. I stopped scraping and paused for several seconds.

"You haven't heard?" Mary asked, when she saw my expression.

I shook my head.

"This week's supply of meat was stolen from the freezer."

"When? Who?"

Mary shrugged. "Don't know, but Gram discovered it late last night when she went to thaw the stew meat. The Professor works on a shoestring. Never a dime left over from week to week, and replacing the meat supply for a week for about eighty of us will be pretty expensive."

"What about the fried chicken we had for dinner today?"

"Set down to thaw in a cooler. They missed it."

"But who else lives out here?"

"That's just it. Camp Jericho covers about a thousand acres. No one else lives anywhere near here."

I drew my brows together and thought of the late-night drive into camp. Nine miles of nothingness.

"That's why the Professor didn't meet your bus. Aunt Lisa was able to get a call out on the cell phone to a friend who found him at the bus station. Your uncle found Ruben and asked for a favor . . . and well . . . you know the rest."

At the sound of the bullhorn, I jerked off my apron.

Uncle Jack bowed his head and thanked God for His provision. Biscuits and stew, even without meat, was pretty good. Frances really was a good cook.

The six cabin counselors along with Mary, Frances, Jordan, Aunt Lisa, and Uncle Jack lingered over Sunday night stew. They enjoyed friendly bantering and exaggerated predictions of the escapades of campers.

Yes, I thought. Maybe I'll fit in. *Might be really fun.*

Greenwood was becoming more and more of a reality. Uncle Jack seemed confident that the sheriff's department would solve the mystery of the gun. The dream was taking shape. But a lingering fear kept the evening from being perfect.

"Does Ruben work here?" I asked.

"Oh my, no. He lives across the border in Ciudad Acuna. Well, *Ciudad* means 'city.' We just call it Acuna. The Professor buys horses from Ruben."

"He seemed a little . . ." I remembered putting my foot in my mouth earlier about Frances. "A little different."

"Weird," Mary said.

"Yeah." We both laughed, and I reached up high to hang the last pot on a hook above the stove.

I adjusted my cap. "Do we have enough daylight left to take a look at those caves?"

"Sure, unless the Professor calls an early Bible study."

Suddenly we had Jordan's attention. "Let's get the horses," he said.

"Uh . . ." I paused. "I think I'll walk. I need the exercise."

"Yeah, right," Jordan said, and took off on foot in the direction of the stable.

Mary shrugged and smiled. "Sometimes you just have to ignore Jordan."

The fifteen-minute walk to the river was relaxed and friendly. Mary gathered a handful of bluebonnets when we passed the girls' cabins.

We found Jordan, mounted and still, staring at the flat-topped mesa across the canyon. The brown jagged mountains in the distance looked much smaller than they really were.

Jordan called out, "Ever been spelunking?"

"Spelunking?"

"Exploring caves," he said with an air of authority.

"No."

Mary started down a steep trail that led to the river below. "Well, really, these caves aren't much to explore. They aren't deep, and you sure don't have to worry about getting lost. Some of the ancient Indian artwork is interesting, though."

Suddenly two blasts from the bullhorn echoed through the air. "Bible study," Jordan said, and we turned and hurried toward the library.

Later, when the sky was completely dark, and all of Camp Jericho had been asleep for a long time, I lay on my bunk and stared up into the blackness above. *Trust God?* I wanted to trust God. I needed something or someone solid to hold on to. It seemed that in the two years since Dad had died, I'd been floating just inches above reality. *Would going to Greenwood Equestrian High School and someday taking the job Dad had*

had as head trainer settle me into reality and peace? It was too much to think about.

"Don't leave the county," Deputy Cole had said.

"We'll be out in a few days to get your fingerprints," the other deputy had said, making me feel like a common criminal.

I pulled the sheet up over my face and roughly wiped the dampness from my eyes.

Early Monday morning, Quarto responded to my touch and soft words as we stood quietly in the stable. The sound of brisk sweeping above my head brought Mole to mind again. He had come in last night long after Dudley and Jordan had started snoring. I had listened to the soft sounds of Mole struggling to pull off his boots, and then within minutes his peculiar snorts and snores had joined the others.

I glanced around at the long row of stalls, impressed with how clean the stable was. Fresh hay had already been brought to the stalls, and fourteen saddles lined the fence, ready for the afternoon trail ride. Mole, whoever he was, sure kept the place up. I backed away from Quarto's stall and looked up, hoping for a glimpse of the elusive Mole. It was quiet up there now.

The tack room, a lean-to attached to the stable, held equipment of one sort or another. Wooden pegs supported bridles, leather reins, ropes, and straps. Saddle racks, mostly bare now, stood in a line down the center of the long narrow room. The strong smell of leather and saddle oils filled the air. It was a familiar and comforting presence. If it were not for the nightmare of the gun and the mystery surrounding it, I could feel as at home in the stable as Mole obviously felt.

"Where is everyone?" I asked Frances a short time later.

"Most are in town."

"In town?"

"The Professor has to replace our supply of meat, and the counselors went along to meet and organize their kids. They'll come in on the buses with the campers."

"And Mary?"

"Finishing up craft materials . . . and Jordan's around here somewhere."

After a fast breakfast, I hurried back to the stable to saddle Quarto. This would be a perfect time to explore before the afternoon trail ride.

"Frenchie's gone." I spoke aloud. At the same time, I noticed a saddle missing from the lineup on the fence.

Quarto was a trainer's dream—fast, responsive, and smart. I spent the next couple of hours getting familiar with the trails that Quarto had already covered hundreds of times. We eventually came out near the field of bluebonnets. Frenchie stood in the distance, motionless, head down, waiting. *Jordan must be in the canyon,* I thought.

I was turning Quarto toward the stable when I heard Jordan call. "Hey, wait up."

I dismounted and dropped the reins.

"Ready to go spelunking?"

"Sure."

"Really, not much to explore," Jordan said, almost apologetically. "None of these caves are deeper than twenty or thirty feet. But, further down the canyon are some pretty impressive caverns. We let the campers go in these shallow caves all the time."

I began to notice the difference in Jordan's disposition. He was not the same sullen guy who shuffled, head down, across the floor of the pavilion yesterday.

I tried to act casual and unimpressed when we entered a cave on hands and knees. Jordan continued a running monologue, like a regular historian, as we entered a larger chamber where we could easily stand, and then we dropped to hands and knees again to squeeze through the more narrow places. West Texas cave dwellers actually made their homes in these very caves. I imagined a father building a fire just outside the mouth of the cave and then going down to the river to fish for their supper. I imagined a mother, deeper in the cave, making a bed of soft animal skins for her children.

The air was cool, and recent signs of life were everywhere—dozens of footprints from kids of all sizes and hundreds of initials carved into the granite and limestone walls. *I can't wait to see the really big caves,* I thought.

A short time later we sat on large rocks with Quarto and Frenchie grazing nearby.

"Pretty scary yesterday," Jordan said, without taking his eyes off the mountains.

So that's why he was suddenly Mr. Nice Guy. "Yeah," I answered.

"Just for the record, I don't think for a second that you put that gun there."

"Thanks."

"Well, just try to forget it," Jordan said, as he removed leaves from the hanging branch of a cottonwood tree.

We were silent for several moments. *So what's going to happen next?* I wondered.

Without taking his eyes from the pile of leaves, Jordan cleared his throat and slumped a little. "I have a confession to make, Tony."

An uncomfortable silence followed, while Jordan seemed to be searching for a way to begin. He glanced at me and grimaced as he brushed the pile of leaves from his jeans. Suddenly Uncle Jack's bullhorn sounded once, and we jerked to attention.

"The buses are back," Jordan said, without much enthusiasm.

A confession? I wondered, but the moment was over. Jordan was gathering Frenchie's reins, ready to meet the campers.

I heard shrieks of laughter and general chaos before I topped the hill above the field of bluebonnets. Jordan was already out of sight. I pulled back on Quarto's reins. "Whoa, boy." The horse stood motionless while I looked over the scene in the distance.

Two old yellow school buses were parked near the pavilion. Dark lettering on the side of the buses read *Del Rio Community Church,* and underneath, faint lettering of years past read *Val Verde County Public Schools.* Campers were leaving the buses slowly, struggling with bags and equipment, cameras, volleyballs, swim fins, and even a tennis racket.

It's probably a twenty-mile hike to the nearest tennis courts, I thought, and then laughed.

David, Dudley, and Tyler gathered their campers in separate groups on the east side of the buses. They called out names and gave instructions. With Sabado at her side, Mary moved from group to group with a clipboard. Rose and her campers were already walking toward Quarto and me. Shrill laughter and high-pitched giggles filled the air.

"Girls," Rose called out over the commotion, "this is Tony. He's our riding instructor."

The girls glanced my way and then admired Quarto as they walked toward their cabin—home for the next five days.

Fifteen minutes later, after settling Quarto in his stall, I joined Mary and Jordan in the kitchen.

Uncle Jack gave one long blow on the bullhorn. "Five minutes," Mary translated. She tossed me an apron while I washed my hands. It seemed that one blow on the horn could mean different things.

Campers came pouring in, lining up along the outside edge of the pavilion, chattering and jostling for a position in line, as they examined the building, and each other.

Suddenly, Uncle Jack's deep voice quieted the crowd as he welcomed the campers officially to Camp Jericho. Then, lowering his head, he asked God's blessing on the meal about to be served.

At the amen, I lifted salad tongs, ready to serve trays. Hamburgers were normally the welcoming meal, but late night raiders had changed that when they robbed the freezer. Jordan served spaghetti without meat in the sauce, and Mary put a slice of garlic toast and a cookie on each tray. Frances was already washing pots and pans and had set out newly delivered meat to thaw for supper.

Campers chattered, praised, and complained, as they went through the serving line.

"Oh boy. Spaghetti."

"I hate salad."

"I wanted hot dogs."

"What's our counselor's name?"

"I want to ride the stallion."

"Did you see that dog?"

"Thank you."

I glanced up. "You're welcome."

When I finished the last of my three cookies and washed my tray, I had less than half an hour to get ready for twelve green riders. Jordan had said the campers would be mostly inexperienced. *Where is Jordan? He needs to help saddle the horses,* I thought. The confession came to mind again. *What was it? Would the subject come up again? Did he know something about the gun?*

I walked to the stable and was surprised to see fourteen horses saddled, their halters tied to the rail fence with leather straps. I examined each saddle and bridle. *Not bad. It was a great job. A professional job. It had to be Mole. But where was he? Who was he?*

A shadowed movement caught my eye. Mole. He was leaving the back of the stable, his small hunched figure shuffling through fresh hay, his arms full of equipment. I caught myself just as my mouth opened to call out, "Mole." *Was that his real name? Did everyone call him Mole? Was it a nickname?* Sunlight glinted off the top of Mole's mostly bald head, and at fifty feet, I couldn't decide if his age was closer to thirty or fifty. He was a mystery.

A shuffling of horses' feet and the sound of their general agitation drew my attention to the far end of the row of horses. "Hey," I called out. "Move back."

"I'm gonna ride now," a bold young camper announced.

"Move back," I called much louder, moving quickly toward the camper.

The small boy's blond hair stuck out in all directions, and his face showed signs of his lunch. Reluctantly he moved back a step or two.

"I signed up to ride a horse," he said. "I'm Charles. I'm the first one on the list."

"Good. I just don't want you to get squashed. Never come up behind a horse like that. He can't see you from that angle, and if you startle him, you could get kicked."

Charles bit his lip and took another step back. "Which horse is mine?"

"Ever ridden a horse before?" I asked, sure that Charles had not.

"Sure, lots of times."

I ignored this and looked around for Jordan. During the almost ten minutes that it took for the campers to drift over to the stable, I'd cautioned Charles three or four more times as he annoyed the horses and then the other campers.

"Your shoes are wet," I said, hearing the squish, squish of Charles's sneakers.

"I went down to the river."

"Did your counselor go with you?" I asked, surprised.

"Well, he came and got me," Charles said, sounding disappointed.

Jordan showed up at the stable with the last camper. Those not riding had signed up for crafts or swimming or volleyball this hour. I was beginning to wish that Charles was playing volleyball.

"Okay, guys, listen up." I began my rehearsed speech. The four girls and eight boys seemed eager to mount their horses. I started with general safety rules and then pointed out the parts of the saddle and bridle.

After a five-minute monologue, I suddenly stopped. "Where is Charles?"

The campers glanced around and shrugged, while Jordan and I began calling and looking. Barn cats scampered out of the way.

Several minutes later, after searching the stable, stalls, and loft, I found Charles in the tack room, mounted on Uncle Jack's saddle, which rested several feet above the ground on a wooden rack. His wet shoes hung far above the stirrups.

I forced myself to stay pleasant. I bit my tongue hard and then said, "Please stay with the group."

Charles shrugged, as though he had a choice. "Sure." He swung to the dirt floor with a thud.

Half an hour later, after a tedious job of helping all twelve campers mount their horses, some from platforms made to help small riders, we slowly began moving toward the trail. Quarto led the way, his obedient spirit and calm nature making him a treasure on hoofs. Charles, happy to be almost first in line, rode behind me. Jordan trailed last, watching for problems.

"Let's take that trail," Charles said, kicking his horse.

The horse stopped suddenly, causing the twelve riders behind him to stop also.

"Keep the reins loose, remember?" I felt a slight headache coming on.

A dozen times during the next half hour, I had to remind Charles, "Keep the reins loose," as the line of horses stopped behind him.

The eleven other campers were quiet, sometimes talking softly to each other and watching for Charles to jerk his reins again.

We entered a clearing and saw Mary in the distance. Her group of campers was busy with some art project at the tables under the pavilion. She waved.

Back at the stable an hour later, Jordan and I helped the campers dismount.

Charles was radiant. "I want to go again."

Not on your life, I thought. "Not today," I said. Charles smiled broadly and hurried away.

Great, just great, I thought, and then heaved a sigh. *There must be an easier way into Greenwood. Would I be allowed anywhere near there after this summer?*

The mystery of the gun brought the dark cloud again.

CHAPTER
5

At 2:30, the second group of campers gathered for their first trail ride. Some carried sand candles still warm from the mold, some were hot and sweaty from an hour of volleyball, and a couple had wet hair and carried towels, a sure sign of a dip in the river.

Forty-five minutes later, a quiet, orderly line of riders entered the clearing across from the pavilion. Jordan and I both stifled a laugh. With at least fifteen campers sitting around tables, Charles sat perched on top of the table, hovering over his can of wet sand, working fervently to shape a mold for the hot candle wax. Mary looked up and gave a slight frown and a helpless shrug.

Later, the supper line moved with no complaints. Campers, many pink from several hours in the sun, were ready for a more relaxed activity.

"Look." I nudged Jordan.

Uncle Jack sat near the end of the row of tables with Charles at his elbow.

"He always gravitates to the needy ones," Frances said, setting down her tray and pulling a folding chair up to the end of the table.

"Camp meeting in the big rock building in fifteen minutes," Dudley announced as campers carried trays to the kitchen and then scurried away from the pavilion.

"Camp meeting?"

"Like church," Jordan said, tying a garbage bag.

"Coming?" Mary called. She and Sabado took several steps toward the library.

"Maybe later," I answered. *Church on Monday night? I don't think so!* "I'll stay here and help Frances."

I worked almost twenty minutes, cleaning tabletops and sweeping the pavilion, while Uncle Jack's welcoming speech boomed clearly through the open windows of the library. *With a public address system like this, not a coyote or an armadillo this side of the canyon will miss a word,* I thought. Uncle Jack's opening prayer included thanksgiving for a day of safety. He asked God to work in the heart of every camper, and then he reminded God that the future of the camp was in His hands.

Wonder what he means by that? I paused in my work and stared in the direction of the big rock building.

"Coming?" Frances asked.

"Uh . . . maybe in a while." I sat on a bench with my back to the table and shoved my elbows behind me, resting them on the wood planks.

Lively camp songs—choruses I hadn't heard in several years—echoed from the library. It sounded like a fun place to be. I closed my eyes and listened, remembering my one camp experience the summer before our family moved to Oklahoma City. A summer with no problems, no grief, and no guilt. A summer when I first remember clearly hearing a gospel message, and now, I suddenly remembered my deliberate decision to ignore the message.

I abruptly opened my eyes and leaned forward trying to remember. *Why? Why didn't I answer the youth minister's call to repent of sin and make Jesus Lord of my life?*

"Close your eyes." Aunt Lisa's silvery voice echoed from the rock building, "Let the Lord speak to your heart."

I held my eyes wide open while Aunt Lisa sang the first verse of a familiar hymn. "My hope is built on nothing less than Jesus' blood and righteousness . . ."

"Here, boy," I said, suddenly distracted by Sabado. For several moments I gave Sabado rough pats and strokes of affection, and then he lay quietly at my feet.

My attention was drawn back to Aunt Lisa as the final chorus filled the air. "On Christ the solid Rock I stand, all other ground is sinking sand; all other ground is sinking sand."

The music made me strangely uncomfortable, and I thought again, *Why didn't I answer that call?*

The darkening sky held the faint outlines of changing clouds. I stared, unfocused. *I could use a solid rock right now.*

After a few moments of shuffling, coughing, and momentary muffled chatter vibrating over the public-address system, Dudley began the evening camp meeting message. I patted my thigh, inviting Sabado up for more attention. The dog responded immediately.

In the faint evening light, Uncle Jack walked toward the pavilion. He nodded a greeting and joined Sabado and me, sitting, like me, with his back resting against the table, elbows shoved back for support.

A mosquito landed on my ear, and I slapped it hard. "Any word from the sheriff?"

"Not yet. Try not to worry." Uncle Jack hung his head back and looked up into the sky. He reminded me of Dad again. After a long period of silence, Uncle Jack said, "Tell me about Greenwood."

A flood of memories rushed in. "Well . . ." I hesitated, not sure what Uncle Jack really wanted to know. "It's a private high school and horse training academy. Dad had just taken over as managing trainer."

"And now you hope to win a scholarship to attend as a student there?"

I nodded and took a shuddering breath before I leaned forward and laced my fingers tightly together.

"You've been riding most of your life, I guess."

"No, not really." Visions of my accident filled my mind. "One of Dad's horses kicked me the day after I turned five. Broke my collarbone and fractured some ribs. I was in the hospital for weeks."

Uncle Jack nodded. "So, when did you start to ride?"

I took a deep breath, glanced over at Uncle Jack in the growing darkness, and murmured, "The day Dad died."

Uncle Jack moved his elbows from the table, leaned forward, and lifted his right boot up over his left knee. He stroked his moustache with two fingers. "Can you tell me about it?"

I shrugged and struggled for emotional control. "Dad surprised me with a horse about a week after he took over at Greenwood. I was as scared as the day I got kicked. Wouldn't have anything to do with the horse. Insisted that he take him back. Dad was returning the horse when a semi forced him off a bridge. It's my fault that Dad died."

Uncle Jack was visibly moved. It was obvious that he hadn't heard the story before. "Andrew would never blame you, Tony." He lightly rested his big arm across my shoulder.

"Yeah, I know Dad wouldn't blame me, but I blame myself."

"Well, Tony," Uncle Jack gave a sad smile, "always remember that God—"

"There you are, Professor. I been lookin' for you," Charles said, appearing from the darkness.

With a quick, affectionate slap on my back, Uncle Jack nodded and took Charles's hand. He placed his big Stetson on the small blond head and turned toward the library.

"I just turned around, and you were gone," Charles said from under the hat.

Later, long after the lights were out, I heard Jordan shifting restlessly in the bunk across from mine. Again the mysterious confession came to mind. Would the subject come up again? I was intensely interested, but determined not to ask. As often happened though, my intentions didn't define my actions.

"You were saying something about a confession . . ." I bit my tongue, annoyed with myself.

Jordan was quiet for an uncomfortable period of time before I heard him get up and walk toward the window. "Yeah . . . I just . . . I mean, I was . . ." Jordan struggled for words, making me wish again that I'd kept my mouth shut. "I guess I was jealous and mad when I heard you were coming. It was like you were taking my place." Then he hurried to add, "Dumb, I know. And, well . . . I just wanted you to know that I sure don't feel that way now. You're okay."

"Oh, uh . . . sure. No problem." It was an awkward, wavering response. I abruptly changed the subject. "Say, what did Uncle Jack mean tonight when he was praying? Something about the future of this camp being in God's hands."

Jordan stretched out on his bed again. Moonlight faintly flickered across his reddish-brown hair and blemished face. "Yeah. The camp is in big trouble. A five thousand dollar balloon payment is due in September. The bank can foreclose on the whole thousand acres if Dad doesn't come up with the money."

"Balloon?" I scratched my mosquito bites.

"A bigger than usual payment. The final payment. It was in the contract years ago."

"Can't he sell off a few acres for the money?"

"Nope. That was in the contract too."

We were silent for a long while. Eventually Jordan's breathing became a soft snore. I listened to faraway screams echoing across the canyon and thought how simple the life of a coyote must be.

Early Tuesday morning, with Jordan still asleep, I made my way to the shower shed. Without intending to, I found myself humming the chorus of the song Aunt Lisa sang last night.

I tossed my towel across a low support beam, when out of the corner of my eye, a glimpse of black and yellow flashed into my consciousness. With a gasp and flailing arms and legs that tried to move faster than my body would go, I firmly smacked my forehead on the low wooden beam. A snake . . . coiled, ready to strike. A snake. Shiny and still. A snake . . . a rubber snake. A black and yellow fake snake had my heart rate up in the rafters.

I heard a sudden burst of laughter as Jordan stepped into the open doorway.

"You fell for that old trick?"

I smiled a little, feeling foolish.

Later, nearing the stable, I slowed my pace, lightly fingering the bruise on my forehead.

"Here you go," Frances said to Mole, as she handed him a tray. Mole belched rudely and begged pardon. *What service. So that's why he didn't eat with the rest of the camp.* Frances sped away on her silent, battery-operated golf cart. Then I glanced over at Mole and was caught by a cold stare. Mole held my eyes for several moments before he turned and walked away without speaking.

"Strange old guy," I murmured. Must have slept here last night.

"What happened to you?" Dudley asked a few minutes later, gesturing toward the bruise on my forehead.

"Rubber snake in the shower," I answered as I filled my glass with milk.

Dudley refilled his coffee cup and lowered his voice as he said, "At least you didn't wake up this morning with red toenails."

It was my turn for a snicker. "I'll take the bruise over the paint job."

Morning camp activities included three-legged races, egg on the spoon races, and numerous skill competitions. Later in the morning, each cabin took time for a brief devotional and then worked on short skits to be presented at one of the evening camp meetings.

I watched Dudley and his twelve campers walk toward their cabin as I swept breakfast crumbs into a pile. Mary and Jordan wiped down tables, and Frances started lunch. Kitchen activities almost never stopped.

"We have time to explore the big cavern, if you want," Jordan said casually.

"Sure." I was glad that I wasn't expected to supervise egg races.

"Hold on a minute," Jordan called, and then walked to the golf cart out behind the kitchen. He returned a moment later, his face trying to stifle a smile, and handed me a light brown wide-brimmed hat, with a snakeskin band. "This is one of Dad's."

First Uncle Jack's boots, and now Uncle Jack's hat. "Thanks. Thanks a lot."

"Dad killed the rattler," Jordan said, gesturing to the band.

I tossed my cap on the table, flung my hair back from my face, and gently settled the cowboy hat in place. A perfect fit. "Thanks," I said again.

"Want to check out the caves?" Jordan called to Mary.

"Can't. Got craft materials to cut out."

A short time later, with hands full of feed, we walked out into the paddock to catch our horses. Frenchie and Quarto willingly accepted their halters. After a brisk brushing, I put the saddle pad and blanket on the horse's back, well forward against the withers, and then pushed it backward until it was in the right position, being careful not to lift any hairs. I set the saddle in place over the blanket and passed the girth straps under Quarto's belly and buckled them to the billets beneath the outer flap of the saddle. Then I slipped the bridle in place, adjusted the straps and latches, and attached the reins.

I remembered the very first time I had saddled Guardian. Guilt and anger smothered my fear. Determination to ride the big stallion overcame even the drenching grief that threatened to choke the breath from me.

"Wanna go for a ride?" I spoke quietly to Quarto, rubbing his soft muzzle.

"Ready?" Jordan sat mounted with his reins in his hand.

I nodded and reached down to tighten the girth straps once more before I lifted my left boot to the stirrup. My full weight rested momentarily in the stirrup as I swung my right leg over the horse and gently lowered myself into the saddle. "Good boy," I said, patting Quarto's neck.

It was the dust that first caught our attention. The Val Verde County patrol car left the cleared, graded road and turned onto the rutted ground near the stable. Uncle Jack followed on Colonel, well behind the settling dust.

"Just a few questions," Deputy Cole said.

I dismounted and waited for Uncle Jack to join us.

"Good news?" Uncle Jack asked a few moments later.

"Well, Professor, could be. The gun was pretty well wiped clean, but we did get one print. Traced it to a convenience store holdup in San Angelo last week."

"Well good." Uncle Jack rested his big hand on my shoulder.

"That still doesn't explain how it got in Tony's bag," the deputy said.

So I'm still in trouble. That old familiar surge of anger flashed through me, and my hands formed tight fists. I deliberately let my shoulders slump a little, and then my hands relaxed.

"Also," the deputy said, stepping close and laying a hand on my shoulder, "there's the little matter of your probation."

I felt my face flush hot.

"What have you come up with?" Uncle Jack asked.

Deputy Cole reviewed a handful of notes. "Your bus went through San Angelo about ten o'clock Saturday night. Do you recall leaving the bus at that stop?"

I squinted my eyes and pressed my lips together, thinking. "Yes, I think so . . . yes, yes, I did. They said it might be the last break before Del Rio."

Deputy Cole nodded. "Everyone get off there?"

"No, some were sleeping. You think someone put the gun in my bag at that stop?"

"Could be. One passenger apparently gave a false name and address. We're checking on that. Could even have been planted once you got here."

Uncle Jack shook his head. "There's no one else around here for miles in any direction."

I cleared my throat and hesitated, "Well, uh, I'm pretty sure I saw white smoke from a campfire a mile or so away, just as we pulled into Jericho Saturday night, . . . but . . . it was Sunday morning by then."

Uncle Jack looked startled. "You sure?"

"Fairly sure. I just thought of it."

"I'll ride out and check around," Uncle Jack said.

"No, Professor. I'd rather you didn't." Deputy Cole spoke with sudden force.

The brisk tone startled even Uncle Jack. "I think I can handle—"

"I know, but it's best if you don't. Just stay out of the woods and report anything unusual." The deputy spoke like a man with authority who was used to being obeyed—even by Uncle Jack.

"Oh, Professor. Thought you'd be interested in this." Deputy Cole handed Uncle Jack a newspaper clipping and then started the patrol car and left in a fog of dust.

Uncle Jack read silently and then handed me the scrap of newsprint and walked away.

Late Wednesday evening, two men held up the Handy Foods Convenience store on Highway 27 outside San Angelo. The pair held a clerk at gunpoint and kept him blinded for several minutes with what appeared to be a silver laser light pointer attached to a leather cord. They left with an undetermined amount of cash. Sheriff's deputies immediately put out an all-points bulletin for the arrest of the men.

I pushed the clipping deep into my back pocket.

CHAPTER

6

"What happened to spelunking?" Mary asked when I joined her at the pavilion.

"Deputy Cole came and took up half our time, and then Uncle Jack sent Jordan to help with three-legged races."

Mary offered a pair of scissors and a stack of colored construction paper. "Cut these out for me?"

"Sure."

"So, what did the deputy say?"

I repeated the discussion and ended with a long sigh.

Mary was quiet for several minutes and then leaned closer and lowered her voice. "Did they question Mole?"

I shrugged and shook my head no. "Why?"

"Uh . . . no reason."

I searched her face. "Why?" I asked again.

Mary shifted and glanced around. "I heard Gram talking to Aunt Lisa. Mole has a police record."

"He does?" I said, much too loudly.

"Shhh . . ."

"Someone should tell the deputies."

"They know."

"Don't let it stick," Frances said, minutes after calling me to help in the kitchen.

I stood, stirring a huge pot of chili and thinking. *So, Mole might have planted the gun. What motive could he possibly have had? Surely not jealousy, like Jordan had confessed. And what had Mole done to earn a police record?*

"Faster."

I glanced at Frances and stirred vigorously.

The afternoon trail rides were uneventful, except for Charles's ceaseless chatter and frequent starts and stops. The evening meal and cleanup chores were becoming routine, and by late evening, I was settled back against the picnic table again, stroking Sabado, and letting myself enjoy the choruses echoing across the grounds of Camp Jericho.

"Why would Mole plant a gun in my bag?" I murmured out loud. Distracting thoughts kept coming. *How could it be related to that convenience store holdup? Why hasn't the deputy questioned Mole? . . . or has he?* My mind was miles away while Dudley's voice filled the air at Jericho.

Wednesday morning, after searching cabinets and storage boxes in the kitchen, Jordan said, "Couple of apples will have to hold us till lunch." It was early—half an hour before Frances would start breakfast. We were determined not to be distracted from exploring the big cavern today. With more than five hours until noon, we had plenty of time. Deputy Cole had said to stay out of the woods . . . but the canyon wasn't the woods.

The field of bluebonnets glistened with early morning dew and the horses moved quietly, parting the flowers like waves in a shallow lake. The girls' cabins were quiet, the weak sunlight not yet working its way through the dense branches of the pecan trees.

We rode silently along the top of the gorge for more than a mile, weaving around patches of cactus and dense brush, before dismounting. We removed the bits from the horses' mouths and tied their halters to the branches of a mesquite.

"How much farther?"

Jordan looked down at the river. "One cave is right below us. The biggest cavern is almost a mile farther down. We'll have to walk from here."

I followed Jordan and made my way down the sloping side of the canyon, grabbing hold of greasewood and sage to keep from slipping.

Suddenly Jordan stiffened and froze in place, his eyes intently staring ahead.

I stood motionless for several moments. My eyes searched for a reason for the silence.

"See 'em?" Jordan whispered barely above a breath.

My eyes explored the side of the canyon but saw nothing. "See what?"

"Snakes."

A shiver ran through me as I frantically tried to find the snakes Jordan was watching. "Where?"

"See that tall cactus? About thirty feet straight ahead?"

I nodded.

"Look about three feet to the right. Rattlesnake on that flat rock."

My head and neck stretched forward, and I squinted my eyes, trying to focus on the rattlesnake that lay coiled on a large gray rock its same color.

"Can't believe you saw him from here," I whispered, thinking how close to the trail the snake was.

"You're in for a show," Jordan whispered. "Look just beyond the rock about another foot or two."

I let out a soft gasp. Another snake, about five feet long, shiny black with yellow patterns, moved slowly toward the rock.

"That one's a king snake," Jordan whispered. "If he's lucky, he's found breakfast."

We watched silently, mesmerized, as the king snake continued to move toward the rattler, and then wrap itself tightly around the rattler and squeeze the life out of it. When the rattler began to struggle, the king snake's teeth sank deep into its victim. With the prey still struggling, his rattles vibrating, the attacker eventually relaxed its coils, unhinged its lower jaw, and began to swallow the rattlesnake headfirst.

I shut my gaping mouth. "I've never seen anything like that in my life."

"I've seen it twice before . . . with Dad. Pretty awesome, huh."

We stood another fifteen minutes, watching as two snakes became one. One bulging, fat snake.

Shaken, but thrilled, I stayed close to Jordan as we looked for the entrance to the cave.

"This one is not so deep, but it has some great drawings all over the walls. Real Indian stuff."

I looked around, waiting to follow Jordan, but seeing no cave.

"You're standing in the entrance," Jordan said, and then laughed.

He pushed aside scrub and sage and then stooped down and disappeared into the side of the canyon. The entrance to the cave was less than three feet high and only shoulder wide. I was leaning down to follow, when Jordan came out again in a fast crawl.

"P-u-eeee," Jordan gasped. "You'll never guess what's in there."

I took a few quick steps down the side of the canyon, thinking of the snakes.

"Rotting meat," Jordan said. "Lots of white butcher paper and almost a week's supply of meat. Nothing we can do about it right now. The thief is probably long gone. Come on; there are five or six more caves before the big one, and then we'll go tell Dad."

I hesitated. "We need to go tell Uncle Jack right now." I motioned for Jordan to head back, but he was already fifty steps ahead of me on his way to the next cave.

"This one's good, too," he said fifteen minutes later, as he ducked into an ancient Indian cave.

I followed, gave my eyes time to adjust to the dim light, and then began to explore. The entrance immediately opened into a larger chamber more than head high and at least ten feet wide. Its length was about twenty feet, where it ended in a crudely shaped archway that partly separated it from a smaller chamber at the back. The damp interior of the cave was much cooler than the outside air.

"They sure decorated the place," I said, studying the carved etchings of horses, trees, and people that covered the limestone walls.

"This is nothing. Wait till you see the—"

"What?"

"Shhhh . . . someone's out there," Jordan whispered. "Move, move!" We flattened ourselves against the left wall in the small chamber in the rear of the cave. The partial wall of the archway blocked our view of the intruders, but would not hide us from anyone standing to the far right in the larger chamber.

"This ain't safe," a raspy voice said.

"Shut up," another voice, much deeper, demanded.

I pressed my back hard against the wall and tried not to breathe. I felt Jordan's right arm against my own left arm and wasn't sure which one of them was trembling.

"How long this time?" the raspy voice said.

There was no answer.

"I ain't sleepin' here again."

My heart pounded.

"Let's get more food from that camp." The raspy voice sounded nervous.

"I said shut up," the deep voice shouted, making Jordan and me flinch and press harder into the limestone.

It occurred to me that no one knew where we were. To be sure no one stopped us, we had deliberately left early. Another mistake.

Then, in the dim light, I noticed our boot prints on the dusty cave floor. They led clearly through the archway.

Shuffling sounds filled the cave as both of the intruders moved to the back of the main cave, next to the archway, and slid to the dirt.

With the groaning and sliding, suddenly one boot appeared in my view, partially erasing the prints we had left in the dirt. My eyes followed the movement of the boot as it rocked back and forth restlessly. Snakeskin. The boot looked like the black and gray rattler we had seen earlier. The toe of the boot was covered with a small metal plate, shaped like Texas.

Cold silence filled the dimly lit cave as the thieves settled in for what might be a long stay. Jordan and I stood still, almost embedded in the limestone, waiting.

God, I prayed silently, *I don't even know how to talk to You. Help.* I remembered again the summer camp I had attended before we left Wisconsin. The speaker had urged the campers to repent of sin and make Jesus Lord of their lives. *How?* I thought now. *How does a person do that? Why didn't I repent back then?*

Suddenly, a sun-browned hand worked the boot off, leaving a dirty sock resting on the floor of the cave. Then red-and-white plaid shirtsleeves came into view as the intruder rubbed the foot and let out a long, low groan.

"I'm tired, I'm hungry, and my feet hurt," the raspy voice said.

"Shut up. We ain't goin' nowhere till we see that map on Saturday. And if it ain't marked, we still ain't goin' nowhere."

After a while my nose began to itch. It was fierce, almost causing my eyes to water. I wrinkled up my face and tried to force my upper lip to reach my nose. It was a monumental feat of self-control to stand still. *Suppose I have to sneeze? Then what?*

"Where are y' goin'?" the raspy voice asked.

"Just out for air," the other voice said, making the shuffling sounds of getting up and moving.

Distracted from my itchy nose, it occurred to me that this might be a good time to make a run for it. One guy was outside, and the other was without his boots. We could be out of the cave before the barefooted one knew what was happening. Jordan and I together could overpower the other guy, if we had to. After all, even if he had a gun, it would be two against one. But I stayed pressed against the wall.

A large, black spider crawled across the opening that separated the main cave from our small, attached hiding place. I squirmed on the inside and focused on the spider. We might just make a run for it after all. A glance at Jordan let me know I wouldn't be alone if I dashed out of the cave. Without warning, the sudden thump of an empty boot did away with the spider and left the boot partly inside the opening of the hiding place.

Thank you. I breathed easier.

The barefoot freezer thief shuffled up and joined his gruff friend outside the cave.

I scratched my mosquito bites and shifted positions.

Jordan whimpered and rubbed his back and legs. "What are we goin' to do?"

"Just wait, I guess. They can't spend all day in here."

I strained to hear the muffled murmur that came from just outside the cave.

"Something about the governor landing," Jordan whispered. ". . . and a theater."

"Shhh." *The governor?*

For over an hour the two thieves sat just outside the entrance of the cave, talking softly and passing time.

"I gotta sit down. My back and legs are killin' me." Jordan started to slide to the dirt.

"No, we can't take the chance," I said. I rubbed my own back, flexed my shoulders, and stretched as high as the low ceiling would allow.

The thieves settled back again next to the arched partition. They seldom spoke and seldom moved. Eventually, a rustling of cellophane and the strike of a match brought the smell of cigarette smoke.

Jordan turned his head abruptly, making a slight sound as his hat rubbed against the wall of the cave. I held my breath.

When I relaxed enough to breathe, irritating smoke stung my throat. A sideways look at Jordan showed him struggling with the smoke also.

Trapped in a cave, not knowing when—or if—we might be free, forced me to think of my life from a completely new point of view. *What really matters? Most things aren't really important. Even Greenwood seems meaningless right now. There has to be more to living than that. On Christ the solid Rock I stand, all other ground is sinking sand . . . That's it. Making Jesus Lord of my life would mean the security of the solid Rock. I wanted that security more than anything.*

"God." I mouthed the words silently, my heart pounding. "I'm truly sorry for all my sin. I don't know how to make Jesus Lord of my life, but I want to now. Help me, please." It was a deliberate prayer of commitment and repentance, born of fear, but genuine and heartfelt.

I caught my breath—startled—suddenly afraid I'd been humming out loud. *Jesus, a solid Rock.* The thought had new meaning now. A comforting presence engulfed me.

Memories of another church camp flooded my mind. Dad had chaperoned the campers three years ago in Wisconsin. It had been a last-minute change of plans—within an hour of leaving—when one of the other parents had a family emergency. The pastor needed another adult in a hurry. I remembered being surprised at the plans because Dad seldom went to church. I remembered also the altar call that I had ignored. Dad hadn't ignored it. His tear-stained face was one big smile. After that, Dad seemed different, more relaxed and pleasant to be around.

I wondered again how I could have sat through Sunday school and church off and on for years, ignoring the salvation message. I had mechanically gone through the motions of Sword drills and even joined the junior choir once, yet failed to make heart contact with God's Word.

I'm starving, I suddenly thought. We had missed breakfast, and I'd given my two apples to Quarto. We had missed lunch, and judging from the fading light at the mouth of the cave, we were about to miss dinner too. Charles came to mind. He loved to ride the horses. Who else would have taken them out today? Everyone would be worried. Is anyone looking for us yet?

"Someone's out there." The deep voice was a frantic, agitated whisper. A scrambling of feet and legs as the thieves got up had me holding my breath again.

"Look, it's that dog from the kids' camp."

Sabado. Sabado had found us. But would it be to rescue us or just to reveal our hiding place? Were we in for more trouble? My emotions bounced between fear of being found by the thieves and excitement at being discovered by Sabado.

"He won't be alone. Let's get out of here," the deep voice said, and I could almost feel the floor of the cave vibrate as the intruders left like a stampede.

We landed on Sabado with fierce hugs and words of praise.

CHAPTER

7

Colonel stood tied near Quarto and Frenchie at the top of the gorge. "Dad's out looking for us," Jordan said, stating the obvious.

"What happened?" Uncle Jack's normally calm voice erupted with emotion as he topped the gorge and hurried toward us.

Sabado stood watching the demonstrative reunion, as Jordan and I both talked at once, pouring out details of the hours we were held hostage unaware by our captors.

Then Uncle Jack moved between us and threw his big arms across our shoulders. "That must have been terribly frightening."

"Oh, I wasn't scared," Jordan said with a shrug, but the streaks of dried salty dust on his cheeks suggested otherwise.

Uncle Jack walked over to Colonel and removed a bolt-action repeating rifle from a sling. Then he moved some distance from the horses and sent two signals echoing across hills and canyons.

"What are they doing here?" I asked, when we topped the rise beyond the field of bluebonnets.

"Looking for you and Jordan. I managed to get a call out on the cell phone." The two patrol cars were parked near the pavilion, but the deputies were not in sight.

Uncle Jack rode in the direction of the library. "Come on; let's show them you're all right."

Camp meeting was well underway, and enthusiastic singing drowned the clatter of the horses' hooves. We dismounted and entered the spirited meeting room. Abruptly the piano stopped when Mary jumped up and rushed down the aisle, followed by Aunt Lisa and Frances. The six counselors and seventy-two campers smiled and clapped.

"We prayed for you," Charles said. His high-pitched voice rang out above the commotion.

"Thanks. Those prayers were answered." *God is a present help in time of trouble? Maybe Uncle Jack was right.*

Over leftover fried chicken and whipped potatoes, Jordan and I told the story again to Mary and Frances. It was hard not to embellish the details.

"Were you scared?" Mary asked.

"You better believe it," I said. Jordan took another piece of chicken.

"We've been praying since lunchtime. When you two didn't show up, we knew something was wrong."

Deputy Cole and a new Deputy, Collins, appeared in the distance. They walked with a determined pace and with expressions to match. They returned their guns to the patrol cars. "More trouble?" Deputy Collins asked. His tone immediately put me in a defensive mode.

"We were held hostage in a cave all day," Jordan said. "And these guys are planning something when the governor lands on Saturday."

"Well, the governor is in Asia at a conference all week, so they'll be disappointed."

"So," Deputy Collins said, "tell us what happened."

I took a deep breath, bit my tongue, and let Jordan do the talking. Jordan started with the snakes, embellished the part about the rotting meat, and then went on to details of our long hours of standing pressed to the wall in the back of the cave.

Deputy Cole crossed his big arms in front of him. "Did you catch a name?"

We glanced at each other. "No."

"You mean in all those hours in that cave, you didn't once hear a name?"

"They didn't talk much," I said, and then wished I'd let Jordan say it.

"You suppose they had something to do with the planted gun?" Uncle Jack asked, when he joined the group under the pavilion.

"I doubt it, Professor. We're tracing a guy, maybe two, who got on the bus in San Angelo. I think all you got here is a pair of hungry meat thieves." The deputy laughed at what he considered a joke.

Uncle Jack frowned. "You will check it out?"

Deputy Collins shrugged. "Did you see their faces?"

"No."

"Did they threaten you?"

"No."

"Did they prevent you in any way from leaving the cave?"

"Well, not exactly."

"Did they harm you?"

Jordan and I looked at each other and shrugged.

"Not much to check out, Professor. And boys," Deputy Cole abruptly took on a stern tone of voice, "I told you not to go out in the woods."

I had to clamp down hard on my tongue to keep from saying that the canyon wasn't the woods.

"The canyon isn't the woods," Jordan said, in a tone bordering on disrespect.

Uncle Jack laid a hand on Jordan's shoulder, and the reprimand was received.

Long after the lights were out, Mole opened the screen door, and in minutes, his peculiar snores and snorts joined Jordan's. Mole would be gone before daylight, adding to the suspicion and mystery that surrounded him.

I'll just bet it was Mole. I got angry again. *But why? Why would Mole hide that gun in my bag? How could Mole have been involved in a store holdup in San Angelo?* Reason told me that it couldn't be. *But then . . . who? . . . and how?*

I was restless and couldn't sleep. My mind drifted to the cave and my decision to make Jesus Lord of my life. The thought relaxed me, and I realized that I was smiling in the darkness. *Why did I wait so long? Why didn't I make the decision when Dad did?* The question had been a lingering, troubling thought. Then suddenly, the answer was clear. Things were too easy back then. No guilt, no fear, no problems. I couldn't see my need for the solid Rock. I smiled again. In a strange way, I felt glad for the cave experience. I slept.

Aunt Lisa led the lively singing, and Mary played the piano Thursday evening at the final camp meeting. The first group of campers would return to Del Rio and other nearby towns at noon on Friday.

I caught Mary's eye, and her face lit up when I slid onto the back row of the crowded library. Uncle Jack didn't try to suppress his smile as he glanced over and gave a welcoming nod.

After the singing, he walked to the front of the building and praised God for His faithfulness. He prayed for the campers, thanked God for their safety, and once again reminded God that the future of the camp was in His hands.

Ahhh, the mortgage on the property.

Uncle Jack returned to his seat, and Dudley got up to speak. It was an evangelistic meeting that lasted longer than usual and ended with many of the campers praying prayers of repentance and commitment. I watched Aunt Lisa on her knees, tears streaming down her smiling face, as she prayed with a dark-haired little girl.

Before dismissing the group, Dudley explained that God commanded new believers to be baptized as a symbol of His death, burial, and resurrection, terms that he had explained earlier in the evening. Those wanting to be baptized were to join him at the front of the library.

Without hesitation or embarrassment, I walked to the front of the building and stood with Charles at my elbow.

Friday afternoon was quiet at Camp Jericho. Mary and Jordan and I sat in the shade of a cottonwood, looking down at the river. My hair was still damp from the baptismal service. I picked leaves from a low hanging branch and then dropped them absent-mindedly to the grassy blanket. Long sighs expressed the boredom and frustration we felt.

"It isn't fair," Mary finally said. "They're just going to let those guys—"

"I've got it." Jordan pounded his fist into his open palm and then jumped up, pacing. "I've got it. *Governor's Landing.* Governor's Landing. It's a park over on Diablo East at Lake Amistad. The amphitheater's there. Remember?" Jordan grew more excited. "They said something about a theater."

"Right," I said, "and a marked map."

"Saturday."

"Well, it sure won't do any good to tell the deputies," Mary said.

"We could tell Uncle Jack."

Jordan shrugged. "Dad would have to report it, and they'd ignore it."

We sat, discouraged, quiet.

"If the map is marked," I said slowly, "they do . . . something. If the map isn't marked, they wait in the canyon."

"Right."

"What map?" Mary asked.

We shrugged.

"What if we got there first and took the map, or changed it, or something?" *Was I grasping at straws?*

"And how are we supposed to get to Governor's Landing?" Mary asked.

Jordan looked up and brightened. "We'll ask Dad to drop us there at the beach for the day. He goes into town for supplies every Saturday."

"Good," I said. "Then . . . then . . . we'll just play it by ear."

Early Saturday, the red Plymouth Voyager started the long, slow roll over the nine miles of ruts and rocks. We were quiet, hesitant to express our thoughts in the hearing of Uncle Jack, and aware that the deputies would get a good laugh out of our plans.

"Have fun and stay together," Uncle Jack said an hour later when he let us out near the main gate at Governor's Landing. "I'll be back here at four o'clock."

The van pulled away, leaving us standing in a wide reception area with hundreds of park visitors drifting in every direction. Little kids squealed with pleasure, beach balls rolled across the sand, and lawn chairs and coolers dotted the beach.

"Where to now?" Mary asked, shifting her bag of beach towels. She adjusted her blue-rimmed sunglasses and looked around.

I noticed the amphitheater in the distance and started toward it. "There's got to be a map around here somewhere."

Jordan hurried to catch up. "Let's just hope we find it before they do."

For over an hour we wandered around the park, checking snack pavilions, rest areas, theater entrances, and the numerous boat docks that lined the west side of the park.

"Why don't we just ask?" Mary finally said.

"Map?" the park ranger repeated a few minutes later. "Sure, out there at the entrance, tacked on the wall of the welcome pavilion."

The same entrance we had come through an hour earlier was covered with bulletin boards, posters of coming events, park schedules, and a large map of Texas and part of Mexico. We had walked right past the display.

"Here it is," Jordan whispered, glancing around as if we were part of a covert operation. He stood with his finger on the map just below Nueva Rosita, Mexico. The town was circled lightly in pencil.

Mary studied the map. "How do we know those guys haven't already been here?"

"We don't know," I said, taking a pencil and carefully erasing the circle. "But, if they haven't seen it before now, they won't see it at all . . . if we've guessed right."

"So, they were given a signal to go to Nueva Rosita . . . and since the signal's not here . . . they'll go back to the canyon. Right?" Jordan was thinking out loud.

"Well, maybe. But, who'll go looking for them now? The deputies don't believe you," Mary said.

We stood leaning against the wood rail skirting of the pavilion, mulling over the hopelessness of the situation. Mary pulled her long golden braid over her shoulder and lightly ran her fingers down it. She tied and retied the green ribbon holding the end. A ribbon the same shade as her eyes.

"Maybe-e-e . . . ," Mary said, and then paused. "Maybe María could help."

"María? Girls' cabin counselor?"

"Yeah, María will take this seriously, and she's a friend of the best tracker and hunter in a hundred miles."

Jordan slammed his fist into his open palm. "Ruben. Of course. I shoulda' thought of Ruben. He's good, and I mean good." Jordan punched the air a couple of times. "He's helped the Federales in Mexico bring in fugitives a bunch of times."

While Mary talked on a pay phone to María, Jordan and I wandered around the open pavilion, watching the tourists and reading the posters and notices.

A poster advertising the San Antonio rodeo suddenly caught my attention. Barrel racing. Quarto could do that. He's fast, smart, and handles easily. The $2,500 first place prize would help pay the mortgage on Camp Jericho. And— more important to me—a rodeo win would look great on the scholarship application. *Greenwood.* My heart beat faster at the thought.

"She said yes! She'll talk to Ruben," Mary sounded relieved.

Jordan suddenly froze. I automatically tensed up and followed his stare to a stranger standing in front of the bulletin board. The boots. They were the black and gray snakeskin that we had stared at for hours. On the toes were small metal plates in the shape of Texas. Slowly, with great care to act naturally, I raised my eyes to the side of the stranger's face. A clean-shaven, pleasant-looking face, not at all like I had imagined. Jordan and I exchanged glances. Now what? Call the deputies? Hear them laugh again?

The stranger took out a pencil and copied down information from a poster before he walked toward the beach. He didn't seem to notice three would-be sleuths hot on his trail.

We sat at a picnic table in the shade of several palm trees for over an hour, sipping colas and keeping the stranger in sight.

Suddenly, Mary laughed out loud and gestured at a large gathering of men who were settling at tables nearby. "Look, three more pair of the identical snakeskin boots, Texas and all."

Anyone could buy those boots.

CHAPTER

"Where are my garbage cans?" Frances stood with a handful of potato peelings.

"Here, throw those in this plastic bag."

"Why, thank you, Tony, I can't imagine what happened to—"

"Something smells good," Uncle Jack said. He came much too close to the kitchen before he stopped to tie Colonel to a post.

Frances scowled at the horse but kept quiet.

"I thought you might like this, Tony," Uncle Jack said, handing me a small paper bag.

I looked in the bag, and my pulse raced. *Uncle Jack's boots, Uncle Jack's hat, and now Uncle Jack's Bible.*

I searched for words, my finger moving over the monogrammed lettering on the Bible. *Tony Vincent.* "But when did you? . . . I mean . . . how?"

Uncle Jack smiled. "My middle name is Anthony. I was called Tony when I was your age."

"You had this Bible when you were—"

"When I first became a Christian." Uncle Jack took two fingers and smoothed his moustache, reminding me again of Dad. "You've made a life-changing decision, Tony. It's a daily walk, and you'll see God's presence and faithfulness in every page of this book."

"Thanks." *We have the same name. My name . . . our name . . . on Uncle Jack's Bible.* "Thanks a lot."

"You might want to start with the book of John."

Later, after Saturday evening supper, I escaped cleanup duty and headed for the stable.

"You might be the answer to Uncle Jack's prayers," I murmured as I rubbed Quarto's soft muzzle. "Come on, boy."

I led Quarto to the paddock as I continued talking . . . to the horse and to myself. "It's easy, just circle the barrels faster than the other horses." Quarto was a willing mount, responsive to the reins and to my voice. "We'll just walk the course first."

Quarto moved with long graceful strides out into the paddock, walked in front of the first garbage can, and then circled back around it and made a straight line for the second. The cans were set in a triangular pattern. The first two, ninety feet apart, formed the base of the triangle. The third, at a hundred and five feet, stood at the tip of the triangle.

"Easy, boy." I reached down and patted the side of Quarto's neck, continuing to talk softly to him. We circled the second garbage can, going in front of it and then back around and then headed for the third. "Keep it nice and straight."

We walked the course twice and then moved to a trot, going through the routine for over an hour, never changing the pattern. The workout lasted until the moon took the place of the sinking sun. I glanced up and saw Mole crouched, watching from the loft.

Sunday morning I tossed my hat up on the bunk, picked up my new Bible, and headed for the big rock building. I made it to the double doors just as Frances arrived, leaving a trail of dust behind her silent golf cart.

"G' mornin', Frances." It was the first time I'd seen her without an apron.

We joined Rose and Amy, the girls' cabin counselors, on the second row. María was spending the weekend at home. On the front row, David and Tyler had a Sunday look about them, pressed, combed, and hatless. Dudley would be speaking at his church in Del Rio. Mary sat at the piano, playing softly. Jordan and his mother sat next to Tyler on the front row. Uncle Jack stood near the pulpit, looking as if he were prepared to speak to massive crowds of believers, instead of the small assembled group of staff members.

I swept the pavilion after dinner, humming the tune that had become a part of me. Other staff members had drifted away to nap or take care of afternoon chores.

Frances removed her apron, shook the crumbs from it, and hung it on a hook in the kitchen. "You're a good worker, Tony."

I smiled and felt my face flush slightly. "I think I'll go check on Quarto."

It'll take weeks of practice, but I know we can do it, I thought. I led Quarto from his stall, saddled and bridled him, and walked him to the paddock. The garbage cans looked rough and uneven in the hoof-scuffed dirt. A wide rutted trail led from the gate to the first can and then from can to can. Loose dirt lay piled almost halfway up around each of the three cans. Yesterday's practice had been a good start, but the wide path between cans was proof that the pattern had not been consistent and straight.

I dropped the reins and moved each of the cans closer to the gate, keeping the pattern, but leaving room for practice on undisturbed ground.

"Keep it smooth and even," I said, patting Quarto's neck and leaning inside as we entered the pocket around the first can. "Bend, boy, bend and turn, and straighten it out. Good job."

After twenty minutes of hard practice, I suddenly felt watched and turned abruptly, breaking the steady pace we had kept up for several laps. Uncle Jack stood leaning against the fence, one boot on the second rail, his arms, from elbows to hands, resting along the top rail.

"Hi, Uncle Jack."

"Nice work." Uncle Jack took one finger and pushed the brim of his hat up a couple of inches. "What's up?"

I formed my words deliberately while I dismounted. "Well, Uncle Jack, I have an idea."

Over the next several minutes I told Uncle Jack about seeing the poster advertising the rodeo, and the $2,500 in prize money. I went into detail about my plans to practice mornings, afternoons, and weekends. I ended with a hopeful, ". . . so, well, what do you think? It's not enough, I know. But it would help, wouldn't it?"

Uncle Jack took off his hat and ran his fingers comblike through his waves. I'd watched Dad rake through his own hair hundreds of times. I shook free of the thought.

"Have you ever ridden in a barrel race?" Uncle Jack asked.

"No, sir."

"Ever trained for one?"

I shook my head no.

"Neither has Quarto. What makes you think you have a chance?"

"Quarto's fast, and smart. And I watched Dad train for races. I'm sure we have a good chance to win."

Uncle Jack took a step up on the second rail of the fence and then jumped over. "Well, he's strong," he said, running experienced fingers down the horse's gaskin muscles. "Hock is low to the ground." He examined Quarto as if he had never seen him before. "He's three years old . . . ideal age. Bred from running stock."

"Deep heart girth and prominent wither," I said, gesturing to the ridge between Quarto's shoulder bones.

Uncle Jack lifted Quarto's right front leg and examined the hoof and leg muscle, nodding as he thought silently. Then he stepped back several feet and took a hard look at the horse. "Well, I suppose it's possible . . . if you're willing to put in some long hours of practice."

"I'm willing. I want to. Quarto wants to."

"I guess first thing you should do then is ask Lisa for permission to practice with Quarto. He's her horse."

"Oh, sure."

When the horses neared the rock building, Uncle Jack pulled back on the reins. "Whoa . . . we have visitors."

Three hundred feet or so down the dirt and gravel road, parked in front of the pavilion, was a large black Lincoln Town Car. The gray-haired driver stepped from the car, said something to the other man, and took out a map. His light tan suit and flashy multicolor tie seemed out of place in the Texas dust and scrub. His passenger rounded the front of the Lincoln, his white shirtsleeves rolled up to his elbows, and the tip of his green and yellow tie tucked under his belt. Both men wore dark reflective sunglasses and had pale complexions.

Uncle Jack dismounted near the pavilion. "Welcome to Camp Jericho."

I sensed a faint strain in Uncle Jack's voice, a caution that kept me mounted and quiet.

The driver, with a large phony-looking smile, stepped in front of his passenger and shoved out his hand. "Mr. Vincent?"

"Jack Vincent," Uncle Jack said. He offered what looked like a reserved handshake.

"Daniel Cleotelis," the driver said, "and my client, Michael Goodman. Nice place you have here."

Uncle Jack only nodded to acknowledge the introduction.

"I understand that this camp will be on the market by September."

Uncle Jack stiffened visibly. "You understand wrong, gentlemen."

"But the bank said—"

"Forget what the bank said. Camp Jericho won't be on the market."

The driver slowly folded his map and gave a frown and a slight jerk of his head to his passenger, sending him back to his seat. He opened his car door and glanced back at Uncle Jack. "Well, I guess we'll just see about that."

A few minutes later we found Aunt Lisa.

"Twenty-five hundred dollars?" she said. "Can you do it?"

"I don't know, but I'd sure like to try." *It could get me into Greenwood,* I thought.

"Jack, what do you think?"

"Well," Uncle Jack rubbed his moustache, "it's a long shot, but possible."

Aunt Lisa smiled, reminding me of a lady on a magazine cover. Her short, black curls bounced with every move. "Of course then, you and Quarto must try." She picked up her Bible and held it with both hands. "But Tony, don't try it without God's help. It would be a waste of time."

I nodded, aware of how different Uncle Jack and Aunt Lisa were, and also how alike.

"Sunday night stew is even better with the beef," Jordan said later that evening. He filled his tray again and took another biscuit.

Mary set a plate of cookies on the picnic table. "Does Quarto really stand a chance in that barrel race?" Word spread fast in Camp Jericho.

"Yeah, I think so . . . a chance." I'd rather have practiced in secret for a while.

"I have a cousin who's big in barrel racing," David said.

"Pass the cookies," Amy said. "We go to the rodeo every year. Barrel racing is the best part."

Rose pushed her tray out of the way and rested her elbows on the table. "I've lived right there in San Antonio for twenty years, and I've never been to a rodeo."

"You can almost get addicted to the excitement," David said, pushing his silver-rimmed glasses back in place. "Tyler, you ever been to a rodeo?"

"Nope."

"How about you, Jordan?"

"Couple of times."

Sunday evening was a family time for the staff at Camp Jericho. Conversation eventually drifted from the hot topic of the evening to a dozen other subjects. Frances told the group—again—about her trip to Russia and her night in jail after her passport was accidentally switched with that of a known criminal. The Professor and Aunt Lisa described how they met twenty-two years ago at a camp meeting in Wyoming where he was speaking and she was singing. Then the group coaxed Jordan and me into giving details of our cave experience again.

I paused after the part about Sabado and our rescue, "Actually . . . something great happened in the cave that I haven't mentioned." I went on to tell about giving my life to Jesus and repenting of my sin. I had confessed salvation before I was baptized, but I hadn't given any details.

Then, one by one, several others shared details of the how and where of their own salvation experiences. I leaned forward on my elbows, fascinated by the different methods God had used to reach each of us.

Long after the sun went down, and when conversation eventually began to fade, Uncle Jack stretched and yawned. "I'm beat."

"Me too."

"So am I."

Others yawned and slowly began to leave the circle of fellowship.

"G' night."

After an hour or more of restless tossing, I slipped from the cabin and headed for the shower shed. I slid to the concrete floor, leaned back against the corrugated sheet metal wall, and adjusted my Bible so that light from the single bulb fell across its pages.

"Read Psalm 46, verse 1," Dudley had said.

"God is our refuge and strength, a very present help in trouble." *My hiding place. Like the back of the cave. We were in trouble, Lord, and You were there.*

I heaved a deep sigh and thought of the book of John. Uncle Jack had said to start there. I read long into the night, closing my Bible only after my eyes began to blur. *I've been brought to this camp for a reason.* I smiled. *Of course, God knows all about the gun, and He knows who put it in my bag. He has everything under control.*

The next morning faith-filled thoughts faded when I rounded the back of the pavilion and saw a Val Verde County patrol car parked at the far end of the pavilion. *What does he want now?*

Mary and Jordan sat at a picnic table ignoring cold ham and eggs. Frances dried a skillet over and over, her eyes never leaving the deputy.

"Is this really necessary?" Uncle Jack asked.

"Just a formality, Professor. We really don't consider Tony a suspect."

I joined Uncle Jack and Deputy Collins. "A suspect?"

"The unidentified passenger on the bus checked out okay. We're back to square one. This is just official paperwork. Nothing to get all riled up about," he said, opening a black box about the size of a notebook.

I stared at the open box. My lips parted and my mouth suddenly went dry. *Fingerprints. He's going to take my fingerprints.* My jaw clenched tightly shut, and my hands formed tight fists.

"Just relax your hands, son. Let 'em go limp. I'll roll the fingers," Deputy Collins said.

In a stupor, I obeyed. Deputy Collins carefully inked, and then rolled, each finger and thumb on a small square on a stiff sheet of white paper. My vision blurred, and my breathing became deep and deliberate.

"All done. Now that wasn't so bad, was it?" the deputy said. "Go have your breakfast." He smiled and offered me a clean paper towel to wipe the ink from my fingers.

Abruptly I turned, leaving the deputy holding the paper towel, and walked, head held high, toward the stable.

Quarto ran the barrel pattern at a full gallop, tipping two garbage cans on the first run. Like a common criminal. Fingerprinted like a convict. Quarto stumbled slightly, causing me to grab for the saddle horn to regain control. I slowed to a trot and continued to ride the pattern, not bothering to reset the overturned garbage cans.

"Raise his shoulder," Uncle Jack called. "Use your outside rein, and don't lean in so much."

I turned Quarto to the fence and dismounted with a vault before the horse slowed to a walk. "It isn't fair. I don't know anything about that gun, and it isn't fair." My voice was loud, and my face and neck burned.

"Hmmm . . ." Uncle Jack was thoughtful for a moment. "I guess all this took God by surprise."

My jaw dropped as my eyebrows lifted. I shrugged and relaxed some, recognizing Uncle Jack's facetious encouragement.

"They're good cops—friends of this camp—and personal friends. Just let them do their jobs."

I nodded.

"We're leaving to meet the campers. Keep him at a walk or slow trot until we do something about this ground," Uncle Jack said, gesturing toward the ruts and piled-up dirt that had caused Quarto to stumble.

Uncle Jack hesitated as he turned to leave. "Always remember that your horse feels and senses your mood. He'll feel it in your hands, your voice, and the pressure of your legs against his side. If you're tense, he's tense. And, Tony," he said, "You'll never really relax until you're confident of God's presence in your life." He smiled and gave me a light whack on the back.

I nodded again and began to rub Quarto's muzzle and speak softly to the horse. Then, for over an hour, we worked together, moving at a slow trot, correcting mistakes, and perfecting the pattern.

I removed the saddle and rubbed Quarto briskly with a clean cloth until he was almost dry. After that, I walked him in a large circle, allowing the horse to drink water several times until he cooled down.

I checked his feet and sprinkled powder under the fetlocks. Then, with a currycomb in my right hand and a body brush in the left, I started at the top of the neck behind the ears, and with full stiff-armed strokes, brushed away dried dirt and dandruff.

I finished the job with a damp sponge around Quarto's face just as one long blow on the bullhorn echoed across the campgrounds. "They're here," I said to Quarto.

CHAPTER

9

"Welcome." Uncle Jack gave his Monday greetings to the new group of campers, briefly went over the safety rules, and then began to pray for God's blessings on the meal and on the campers.

Suddenly, loud shuffling and heavy breathing and snorting sounds caused me to look up before the "amen." Two campers were struggling for first place in line. The boys, eleven-year-old fifth graders, I learned later, snapped to attention as Uncle Jack—without a pause in his prayer—lifted them both almost off the floor by the neck of their shirts.

I suppressed a smile and squeezed my eyes shut. When I opened them after the close of the prayer—a much longer than usual prayer—Uncle Jack and the scuffling campers were at the end of the line.

"Oh good. Hamburgers."

"More pickles, please."

"The dog's name is Sabado."

"Brad and Frank are at the back now."

"Good."

Several minutes before the campers started taking empty trays to the kitchen, I followed Mary and Jordan to a table and set down my own tray, heaped up with three hamburgers and all the extras. I glanced again down the long row of tables and tried to watch without staring at Uncle Jack talking to the two rowdy campers.

Jordan followed my gaze. "Tall one is Frank. Other one is Brad."

I nodded and picked up a hamburger. Frank was taller than the other campers. His straight black hair hung over his eyes, almost covering the silent scowl on his face. A red-and-white striped shirt covered thin shoulders, and fading bruises covered Frank's arms.

Brad, short and heavy with close-cropped reddish blond hair, was busy giving Uncle Jack his life story. His chunky voice rose above the chatter filling the pavilion, and his smile drew attention to his large, round face.

"Looks like the Professor has already found his calling for the week," Frances said, as she pulled a folding chair up to the end of the table.

An hour later, ten campers sat quietly mounted on their horses, waiting.

"We're supposed to have twelve riders," Jordan said.

"We'll give them five minutes, and then one of us will have to ride out and find Uncle Jack to report—"

"Oh, no," Jordan murmured, and then dismounted.

Brad and Frank sauntered slowly toward the stable from the direction of the narrow path—the off-limits path.

"Where have you been?" I tried not to let my irritation show.

Frank stood with his skinny arms folded in front of him. "The Professor needed our help. He said you could wait."

I let out a snort and shook my head. "Yeah, right! Get mounted."

Getting mounted was a fiasco. With one foot in the stirrup, Frank hopped around following the horse several steps while I grasped for the reins to steady him. At the same time,

Brad struggled to reach the saddle horn. His big smile turned into a frustrated grimace.

"Our horses back home are better than these," Frank said. He kept a fierce grip on the reins.

Brad nodded and watched Frank closely, while Jordan hiked him up into the saddle and shortened the stirrups.

I shook my head and looked at Frank. "You're amazing." I didn't mean it as a compliment. "How old are you?" I asked, as I lengthened the stirrups.

"Fourteen."

I stopped what I was doing, stood up straight, and smiled. "I'm seventy-two."

Frank smiled back.

I went over the safety rules, repeating each point and asking questions. Anything to delay and shorten the trail ride. The campers and their horses were becoming restless, ready to get on with it. Even Jordan was frowning at the extralong safety narrative.

"Know what I hate about this place?" Frank said.

I rolled my eyes and tried to ignore it.

"You teachers think you know it all."

Brad nodded his agreement.

"That did it." I wheeled around in the saddle. "We'll ride in the paddock today."

Most of the twelve riders moaned and mumbled their complaints. Frank grinned smugly. Brad nodded his agreement, although he looked confused.

The ride, circling the paddock, was an ordeal that we were all glad to end. And I was concerned about the mess that the horses' hooves were making. *The rutted ground will make barrel practice nearly impossible,* I thought.

The second and third group of afternoon riders were friendly and followed instructions. The trail rides were fun—even for the guides.

When the horses emerged from the wide trail in sight of the pavilion near the end of the third session, I caught sight of Mary. Her voice was raised and her face appeared flushed, even at a hundred feet away. "I said No!" Mary shouted.

"Keep them here," I called to Jordan as Quarto took off in a lope.

"Tony." Mary was breathing hard. "These guys insist on pouring their own hot melted wax. Frank even forced the can out of my hand." Mary trembled slightly. "Hot wax can be very dangerous."

I wheeled around on the heels of my boots and had to force myself to unclench my fists and breathe deeply.

"Sit down."

"I don't see why we can't—"

"SIT DOWN."

Frank and Brad sank to the bench.

"Apologize to Mary."

"I'll think about it."

"NO. You'll do it now."

Frank turned his head slowly toward Mary and paused. Brad, his brow creased slightly, looked up at Frank as if to gauge his own reaction.

Frank stayed silent. Brad shrugged.

"Maybe we should call your parents to come and take you home," I said.

Suddenly Frank's shoulders slumped. "I'm sorry."

"Me too." Frank's shadow was definitely a follower.

"I'm goin' up to the house to have supper with Mom," Jordan said half an hour later. He turned Frenchie toward home.

I finished drying and brushing Quarto. Mole would care for the rest of the horses. Then I walked toward the staff cabin for a shower and change of clothes before the evening meal and camp meeting.

Suddenly, a glimpse of green caught my attention, and I reached down to pick up a twenty-dollar bill. Then, before my hand touched the bill, it instantly flew through the brush, twisting through twigs and leaves. I heard campers laughing and scurrying off through the off-limits sage and bushes. First a rubber snake, and now a disappearing twenty-dollar bill.

"Guess what I saw on the trail today," Dudley said later, heaping his tray with French fries.

I grinned. "The same twenty-dollar bill that I found?"

We both laughed.

"Actually," Dudley said, turning serious and lowering his voice, "those guys have some real problems—problems that only God can fix."

While Dudley and I finished supper, Uncle Jack sat between Brad and Frank. He talked, smiled, and gave an occasional good-natured poke with his elbow. It was almost sad to see how desperately the boys absorbed the attention.

By the time Frances and I finished kitchen duties, Aunt Lisa's soft soprano voice filled the air at Camp Jericho. I hummed along. When I entered the rear doors of the library, David caught my attention with a nod of his head. I followed the nod and saw Frank and Brad scuffling and laughing.

"Shove over, Frank," I said with a lowered voice, and then I sat between the boys.

Frank instantly turned sulky and turned his face away, but Brad, his head below my shoulder, looked up expectantly with a happy smile. He gave me a poke with his elbow. I remembered Uncle Jack's playful pokes earlier and only smiled in return.

After David and some of his campers led choruses and put on a short skit, they joined the boys on the back row.

"Got your Bibles?" Dudley asked in a booming voice and then adjusted the microphone. Most of the hands in the building went up, some waving their Bibles.

"Great."

Frank's restless fidgeting distracted my attention, and I couldn't help noticing again the bruises on his thin arms. "Problems that only God can fix," Dudley had said. I sat stonefaced, trying to listen, but a flood of compassion was filling me up. Frank was aggravating, but Frank needed help.

I thought of the verse in Psalms I had read that night in the shower shed. "God is our refuge and strength, a very present help in trouble." Frank had big troubles, and he didn't know God was there to help.

I tried to drag my attention back to the pulpit.

"If we confess our sins, he is faithful and just to forgive us our sins, and to cleanse us from all unrighteousness. I John 1:9." Dudley read the Scripture and then went on to tell the campers how forgiven sin could make them free.

I leaned forward and put one foot on one knee and wrapped my fingers around it. I found myself nodding in agreement. Yes, I had felt free since my decision to make Jesus Lord of my life. Free and clean.

Dudley's voice caught my attention again as he read from Psalm 34:18, "The Lord is nigh unto them that are of a broken heart; and saveth such as be of a contrite spirit."

Abruptly I looked over at Frank. A broken heart. Maybe. Sad, for sure. Frank needed Jesus. Of course, all the campers needed Jesus, but I felt a heavy burden for Frank.

Half an hour later, during an altar call that had a dozen campers on their knees, I sat stiffly between Frank and Brad. My heart beat fiercely, and large beads of sweat lined my brow. *What can I say?* I thought almost frantically. *How can I start? Frank needs Jesus.*

I watched Aunt Lisa on her knees on the wood floor in front of the altar with her arm around a sandy-haired camper. She was smiling, talking with her mouth right up to the young girl's ear. *What's she saying?* I wondered. *How does she start?* Uncle Jack was talking to another camper, and Rose and Amy were huddled close to others. I glanced over at Frank and saw him roll his eyes and cross his arms across his chest.

I slumped back. My spiritual boldness was greatly exceeded by Frank's apparent resistance. *Tomorrow night I'll come prepared.*

Tuesday morning, before the sun reached Camp Jericho, I awoke to the creak of the front porch. I managed to focus my eyes in time to see Mole set his straw hat on his slick head, and then I watched him disappear into the darkness. I punched my pillow into shape again and eased my head back down.

I stared into the darkness, suddenly wondering for the first time whether Mom had ever made a commitment to follow Jesus. Strange. I hadn't thought of it before. Then, for the next fifteen or twenty minutes, I mentally wrote and rewrote the letter that God seemed to be prompting me to write.

I left the cabin when the very first traces of pink began to make streaks in the eastern sky.

"You're out early this morning," Uncle Jack said as he approached the stable on Colonel.

"Well, I'm not the earliest bird." I tightened Quarto's girth straps a second time.

Uncle Jack smiled slightly and smoothed his moustache with two fingers. "Every morning Colonel and I make the rounds of the camp before daybreak."

I hadn't known. I nodded, amazed at another little revelation about Uncle Jack.

"Thought I'd get in an hour with Quarto before breakfast."

Uncle Jack dismounted and followed me around behind the stable in the direction of the paddock.

"I'm not getting in nearly as much practice time as I—"

Slowly, with my eyes darting from one side of the paddock to the other, my face broke into a smile.

"You?" I asked, gesturing toward the smooth, freshly graded ground.

"Mr. Molenski."

"Who? Oh!" Mole. Mole had dragged the ground. And the garbage cans were gone. In their place were three barrels. Yellow barrels. 55-gallon drums with a wide orange stripe circling each one.

"This is great, really great," I said.

"We got these barrels a couple of years ago, thinking we'd float a raft out in the swimming area. Never got around to it."

"Got time to watch?" I called as Quarto began to trot the pattern.

Uncle Jack rested his arms along the top rail of the fence and then took one finger and pushed the brim of his hat up a couple of inches. He watched Quarto circle each barrel and work the pattern several times before he called out. "Get his shoulder up."

I instinctively put boot pressure on Quarto's side. The side next to the barrel.

"Good. Now keep your hands low . . . put more weight in the outside stirrup when you make the turn . . . now smooch and cluck . . . good . . . good."

I concentrated on the changes I was making and felt encouraged that Uncle Jack could see ways to improve my style and increase our chances of winning.

"Drive your feet into the stirrups . . . toes up, heels down . . . loosen up and take a deep seat . . . spread your hands evenly on each side of his neck . . . good . . . good . . . good."

After Quarto trotted the course for fifteen or twenty minutes, Uncle Jack called me to the fence. "Good practice. You're making progress."

"I'm ready to take him to a gallop."

Uncle Jack shook his head. "Unfortunately, practice doesn't make perfect, Tony. Only perfect practice makes perfect. I'd keep him at a trot until he's doing it right."

"He's not doing it right?"

Uncle Jack smiled slightly. "Races are won by seconds, sometimes fractions of a second. Look at the path between the barrels."

I looked. "Oh." The wide display of hoof prints between barrels was proof that Quarto was not running a straight course.

"Also, he's squaring off—not bending enough in the turns—and hesitating."

I dismounted, suddenly discouraged. "I've just got to do it."

"You can. You're doing great. Practice small circles to help him bend and flex. In fact, it wouldn't hurt to slow to a walk and just circle each barrel two or three times before you walk to the next one and do the same."

Uncle Jack began to walk away. "Give him half an hour of this and then trot the course again. You'll see the difference."

I glanced up at the loft and saw a hunched form in the open window. "Uncle Jack? Did the deputies question Mole about that planted gun?"

"Who?"

"Mr. Molenski."

"Not that I know of."

"Well . . . don't you think they should? . . . I mean with his police record and all."

Uncle Jack took a deep breath and let out a sigh. "That was a long, long time ago."

Before I could form my next question, Uncle Jack was on his way to the stable.

CHAPTER
10

"You were right. I do see a difference," I said, scooping scrambled eggs onto Uncle Jack's tray. "He's tighter in the turns and seems to know what I want."

Uncle Jack only smiled and nodded. "I'll have some of that sausage too. Oh, Tony, would you mind riding up after breakfast and giving this letter to your Aunt Lisa? And here's one for you."

"Mail delivery way out here?" I asked, looking at Mom's familiar handwriting.

"Once a week . . . or we can pick it up in town anytime."

"Well, you look pretty smug," Mary said when she set her breakfast tray on the table several minutes later.

I folded the letter and stuffed it into my pocket. "Mom says one of the other applicants for the scholarship to Greenwood dropped out—went to another place."

"So, now it's just two of you competing, right?"

"Yep, and this rodeo win will look pretty impressive on my record. I've just got to spend more time with Quarto every day. An hour before breakfast isn't nearly enough. As soon as I deliver this letter to Aunt Lisa, we'll get in another hour."

I sat on Aunt Lisa's porch twenty minutes later. "You visiting too, Sabado?" I patted and stroked the dog.

"Well, Tony. Come in," Aunt Lisa said, suddenly appearing at the screen door.

"Got a letter for you."

"Oh, good!" Aunt Lisa took the letter, examined the return address, and then fanned the air with it for a moment. "Just in time to pay the electric bill," she said, opening the envelope and taking out a check.

"Guess you keep real busy out here writing magazine articles and stuff."

"Yes, and the checks always come just in time. Sit down, Tony."

I'd been inching toward the door, eager to get Quarto back to the paddock for another round of practice before lunch.

"How is Quarto doing with the barrels?"

"With Uncle Jack's help, we're getting better." I told Aunt Lisa about the garbage cans and now the new yellow and orange barrels.

She leaned forward expectantly, listening intently and asking questions. She was easy to talk to.

"So Mr. Molenski dragged the ground for you. I'm glad. Henry has a good heart."

Henry? Mole had a first name?

"Mole . . . I mean . . . Mr. Molenski . . . is kind of . . . I mean he's . . ."

"He's had a hard life," Aunt Lisa said. "But he's been faithful to this camp for almost fifteen years."

"I heard he has a police record." I bit my tongue. I hadn't wanted to say that.

If Aunt Lisa was surprised, or annoyed, she didn't show it. After several moments, she spoke. "Henry was only eighteen.

He and some young friends tried to hold up a bank. A security guard stopped them."

"So they used a gun."

Aunt Lisa nodded.

"Do you think . . ." I looked away and wished again that I had more control of my mouth. "Well, do you think Mole . . . Mr. Molenski . . . could have planted the gun in my bag?"

Aunt Lisa stood up abruptly and took a step back. "Absolutely not. Where did you get an idea like that?"

"Guess I'm grasping at straws," I said. I moved again toward the door.

Aunt Lisa sat and changed the subject. "I hear the staff has a real challenge with a couple of the campers this week."

"Yeah . . . yes . . . actually one camper. Frank. His sidekick is one hundred percent follower. If we get Frank, we'll get Brad." I sat back down when I remembered the altar call last night and my determination to be prepared tonight. "I was wondering, Aunt Lisa . . . about how to . . . well, when you talk to the kids at the altar. You know . . . what do you say?"

"Hmm." Aunt Lisa nodded. "Well, first I say something about how pleased I am for them . . . that they're ready to be serious about Jesus and His plan for them. And then . . . I guess I share the appropriate Scripture—not too much all at once—showing them what God says about their decision to make a commitment to Him." Aunt Lisa reached over for her Bible and wrote down several Scripture references. "If you'll read these several times, you'll soon know them by heart." She handed me the paper.

"Thanks."

"But, Tony . . . God prepares the heart, and He honors His Word in His own time."

"Thanks." I noticed the clock and thought again of Quarto. I took the three or four steps to the door. "You know, Aunt Lisa, I had no idea that my first trip to Texas would turn out to be so—"

"Oh, but this isn't your first trip here, Tony."

I paused, my brows drawn together and my mouth partly open as I struggled for a response. "It isn't?"

"Look." Aunt Lisa opened a drawer and took out a big black and gold photo album.

I hesitated and looked at Quarto tied to the tree just past the front yard. Then I moved back to the chair again.

"Look at this." Aunt Lisa turned to one of the first pages of the big album and put the book on the coffee table in front of me.

I looked hard. Horses and riders. Men and little boys. Then I recognized Dad. I drew the book closer and leaned down. My heart was beginning to beat faster. Dad and . . . and someone . . . on a large black stallion. Next to them were Uncle Jack and a small child on another horse. I pointed to the boy mounted with Dad and looked at Aunt Lisa.

"Yes, that's you. You had just turned three. And there's Jordan and Jack."

"But . . . where was it taken?"

"Your mom snapped the picture about a mile up the canyon. On this property, only we didn't own it yet."

Aunt Lisa's happy face relaxed into a frown for a moment. "I can't imagine living anywhere else."

Before I could respond, Aunt Lisa began turning pages and giving family history with every picture. I squirmed on the inside and glanced out at Quarto several times. Then I caught a quick sideways look at the clock.

Aunt Lisa didn't notice.

Later, Jordan served spaghetti while Mary and I put salad and garlic toast on trays.

"Nothing for you?" Mary called over to David.

"Not hungry," David said, without raising his voice.

Brad leaned over his tray, his chin just inches above his pile of meatballs, while Frank looked around the pavilion, exchanging glares with anyone who looked up.

Frances had said that neither boy had a father. Sad. *I remembered when Dad died. I was probably pretty sulky then too,* I thought. *Sulky, angry and afraid. Really afraid. I'll try to be more patient—patient and understanding.*

The next trail ride turned out to be a test of my good intentions. "Where have you been this time?" I almost said, but suddenly I didn't want to hear the answer.

Frank and Brad mounted their horses while the other campers waited impatiently, hoping for a ride on the trails instead of the paddock today. Only the newly graded ground in the paddock kept me from taking the riders there.

"Frank, relax your grip and give him his lead. He'll stay right behind Quarto."

I glanced back several times to be sure Frank and his shadow were following. Brad chattered constantly, mostly to himself or to his horse. Frank was characteristically quiet, and the other riders talked easily with each other and with Jordan. Near the end of an uneventful ride, we emerged from the trail and into the clearing in sight of the pavilion. Mary waved just seconds before I heard Frank shout. "Kick him hard, Brad."

Suddenly, Frank and Brad raced off past the pavilion. Dust flew in all directions, and the other horses nervously danced and lurched.

I took off in a fast gallop while Jordan helped calm the campers and their mounts.

"Pull back on the reins," I shouted to Brad, who was breathing hard and had tears streaming down his round face. "Whoa . . . whoa . . . sit here and don't you move."

Brad clutched the saddle horn, his knuckles white and his shoulders trembling. Fifty feet beyond the pavilion, Frank lay sprawled in the dirt. His eyes glistened and his chest heaved in and out. His horse was out of sight.

"Are you okay?" I shouted. My heart raced and my head pounded. "You could have gotten yourself killed," I said between clenched teeth and then forced myself to relax.

Frank shrugged and sat up.

"I could lose my job, too," I said, suddenly thinking of myself.

"I feel real bad about that," Frank said.

"No, you don't."

"You're right. I don't."

"What's going on?" Uncle Jack's tranquil presence quickly helped ease the tension.

Later, as Dudley stood to speak, I slipped into the back row in the library, behind Uncle Jack and Frank and Brad.

"Where's David?" I whispered to Jordan.

"Not feeling so good."

"I wondered why he wasn't at supper."

I opened my Bible to the verses Dudley was reading. For the next half hour, Dudley talked to the campers about the importance of a pure conscience.

". . . and having the clean free feeling of having nothing to hide." Dudley spread his hands and then lifted them high.

From my position in the back row, I watched Frank gaze about the auditorium, seeming deaf to Dudley's words. *Come on, Frank. Listen. This is for you!*

Frank focused on the ceiling, and Uncle Jack reached around and rested his long arm behind him.

Dudley read, "Therefore if any man be in Christ, he is a new creature: old things are passed away; behold, all things are become new. II Corinthians 5:17."

See, Frank, I thought, *you can start over. Just like I did.*

Frank stared though the open window.

When Dudley invited campers to come forward and commit their lives to Jesus, I watched Frank for any sign of softening. Frank studied his shoes.

After Uncle Jack left the bench to join campers who had gone forward, my heart began to pick up speed. *Say something. Frank needs help.* I leaned forward ready to whisper to Frank, but then hesitated and sat back. My stomach muscles tightened up, and beads of sweat formed along my hairline. *Say something.* Nothing came to mind.

Aunt Lisa rested on her knees at the altar with a small girl whose short curls were as black as her own. I remembered Aunt Lisa's words earlier in the day. "I tell them how glad I am that they're ready to make this commitment." *Can't use that line with Frank.* I thought of the verses Aunt Lisa had written down. I'd looked them up and even marked them in my Bible. None were appropriate now. Frank simply wasn't interested.

My hands gripped my Bible. My knuckles were white. Abruptly I got up and moved to the aisle where I stood a moment. My heart beat faster. *Do I go forward and share these verses with some other camper . . . or just leave?*

I shoved open the back doors of the library and almost tripped over someone.

"Mo—Mr. Molenski," I said, catching myself on the rail. Mole scramble up from where he had been sitting on the ground listening.

He hurried away into the darkness before I had the presence of mind to say more.

Well, that's just great, I mentally berated myself. *You did nothing for Frank, and you ran Mole off.*

I stood and listened to the soft sounds of Mary's piano above the hum of activity at the altar, and then turned and walked toward the staff cottage, my head down and my shoulders slumped.

"I tried, God."

I looked up at the dark sky. The moon was mostly hidden behind the clouds. "I wanted You to use me . . . but I didn't know what to say to Fr—"

A rustling in the dark bushes startled me from my prayer and spooked my imagination. Another rustling sound caused me to quicken my pace.

All at once the bushes parted and a large furry animal hurdled toward me.

"Sabado. What's the big idea, scaring the life out of me?" I crouched down and roughly patted and stroked the golden retriever. The dog's tail whipped back and forth.

Sabado wandered back in the direction of the library after I climbed up on my bunk and began a letter to Mom—the letter that had been forming in my mind all day.

Later, I had slept only a couple of hours when I opened my eyes—disoriented.

"Tony . . . Tony . . . wake up." Someone was shaking my shoulder and whispering.

"What . . . ?"

"I need you to sleep in David's cottage. I'm taking him to the hospital," Uncle Jack said.

"What?" I couldn't seem to make sense of the intrusion on my deep sleep.

"I'm driving David to the hospital. You need to sleep with his campers."

"Oh." *David's sick . . . I'll sleep with his boys. Ohhhh no! Frank and Brad.* I moaned silently and slid to the floor.

Moments later I sat in the front seat of the red Plymouth Voyager, twisted around to look at David, who sat with his arms wrapped tightly around his middle. His sun-darkened face was pale, and his unruly brown hair looked as if he'd lain awake tossing and turning for hours. David's heavyset broad shoulders lay limp and quivering against the seat back. He looked awful, and I was suddenly wide awake, afraid for David.

"Tony is in charge now, boys. Do as he says. We'll be back as soon as we can." Uncle Jack drove off toward the long narrow road leading to the highway. Twelve hyper campers stood around the porch. I winced at the thought of the bumps and ruts that would shake and hurt David with every bounce. Then I thought of Psalm 46:1, "God is our refuge and strength, a very present help in trouble." *Help David, God, please.*

"Okay, guys," I said, suddenly taking control and using my in-charge voice. "David will be fine. Let's get some sleep."

The campers followed me inside, asking questions and nervously speculating on David's illness.

"We can't sleep," Frank said, "Let's go for a midnight hike in the woods."

"Yeah." A cheer went up. Great idea. "Yeah . . ." they all agreed. "Can we? Can we go on a hike?"

"No way!" I shouted above the commotion. "Go to bed."

Frank stood his ground. "Know what I hate about this place?"

I rolled my eyes. *Here we go again.* "Go to bed."

"You teachers always get your way."

"Right. Go to bed."

"I have survival training."

"No, you don't."

"Yes, I do."

"GO TO BED."

Frank gave up and climbed up onto the high bunk.

I lay back in the darkness and wondered how David would have handled this. I didn't feel so good about it. Eventually the room grew quiet and I slept.

CHAPTER

11

I awoke Wednesday morning to a burst of light and sound.

"Frank and Brad are gone."

"What?"

"Frank and Brad. They're gone. Must have gone on that hike."

"Oooh, nooo." I got up and looked out the window. "Are you sure?"

The other campers shrugged in a see-for-yourself gesture.

"Come on." I headed for the pavilion with my shirttail out and my hair uncombed. I rubbed my chin, suddenly aware that I was well overdue for my weekly shave. So much for barrel practice. Another missed opportunity.

"You're early," Frances said, and then read the look on my face and noticed my disheveled appearance. "What's wrong?"

As I explained the situation, my eyes fell on Uncle Jack's bullhorn hanging from a hook high in the kitchen. I took it down. "Maybe we should get everyone here in case anyone has seen them."

Frances nodded and I sounded the alert. Three blows. Come now.

"What's happened?"

"Why are we here?"

"Is there an emergency?"

Within minutes, campers and staff had gathered at the pavilion.

"No, haven't seen Frank or Brad."

"No, we don't know anything . . ."

Soon after the assembled group drifted back toward their cabins, the red minivan pulled up to the pavilion.

My ten campers greeted Uncle Jack with the news. "Brad and Frank are missing, Professor."

Uncle Jack didn't speak, but looked at me for an explanation. My voice caught in my throat as I tried to explain how I had bungled a simple assignment. Sleep with twelve campers. Now, two were missing.

"How is David?" Frances asked.

"He's okay. Missing his appendix, and he'll be in the hospital a few days, but he's okay."

That was good news, but the immediate emergency was at the front of everyone's mind. "How long have they been gone?" Uncle Jack asked.

"We discovered them missing only twenty minutes ago," I said, grateful that Uncle Jack was back to take over.

"Boys," he said to the campers, "have your breakfast and then hang around the pavilion with Mary and Frances."

Uncle Jack turned to Jordan and me and gave a thumbs up. "Let's get the horses and round up those guys."

A short time later, Uncle Jack and Colonel took off in a lope toward the canyon. Jordan and Frenchie headed toward the area behind the paddock, and Quarto and I began to search the woods behind the boys' cabins.

Half a mile into the thicket, I slowed and dismounted. I stood still and listened, straining hard for any unusual sound.

I stared into the trees and brush for a glimpse of Frank's black hair or the reddish-blond Brad. Black-eyed Susans and Texas mountain laurels dotted the ground as far as I could see. The wind hummed through the tall brush and the few taller trees, and a mourning dove rustled the leaves of the mesquite, reminding me of the living silence I had experienced that first night at the bus stop.

I returned to the saddle and kept Quarto still for several minutes. "I need help, Lord. Your Word says You're a present help in time of trouble. Please bring Frank and Brad back safely." It was a short prayer, but the only words that came to mind.

My thoughts turned to Frank again. *Poor Frank.* The bruises on his arms were hardly more than faint memories, but they were reminders of the kind of home he came from. No wonder he had problems; no wonder he resented leadership; no wonder he resisted the authority of a Heavenly Father. *Dudley was right,* I thought again. *Only God can fix Frank's problems.*

Brad was a different situation. A happy follower being led down the wrong path. Probably Frank stayed close to Brad because their lives at home were similar. I speculated, guessing at motives and wondering how I had become involved in such problems.

Rustling in the tree above and high-pitched birdlike chattering distracted me, and I watched for several moments as two squirrels leaped from branch to branch, causing dried leaves and twigs to rain down.

Slowly, with a lack of clear direction from God, I guided Quarto even farther from camp. I dodged Devil's Head cactus and watched a turkey vulture circle overhead. I shuddered. Maybe Uncle Jack had found the boys by now. It was nearing noon. As I turned to head back, I caught my breath. A white-tailed deer stood less than thirty feet away—watching.

Twenty minutes later, I found Jordan at the pavilion, finishing lunch. "They back?"

Jordan shook his head. "Dad said to stay here and wait for the deputies."

"He called them?" I said, annoyed at having to see the deputies again.

"Had to. Frances said he searched for an hour; then when we weren't back, he took the cell phone with him up the hill. I'm only guessing that he got a call out, but usually, if you ride far enough up the canyon, the static clears."

I thought again about barrel practice with Quarto. Another morning come and gone. "What about trail rides today?"

Jordan shook his head. "David's campers went to Dudley and Tyler. They'll do relay games and stuff around the cabins. Dad wants everyone close right now."

I remembered the fiasco with the horses yesterday when Frank and Brad raced off, and I felt glad for a break today. "We've had a hard time handling those boys."

"We?"

"Me! . . . OK? . . . Me!" My voice rose an octave, and the back of my neck burned. It was true. I had been the one who hadn't been able to handle Brad and Frank—on the trail or in the cottage.

"Dad," Jordan said. He gestured to the horse and rider topping the hill that hid the field of bluebonnets. "And he's alone."

"No sign of them?" Uncle Jack called. He neared the pavilion and then tied Colonel to the corner post.

I glanced toward the kitchen and saw Frances scowling at the horse and the flying dust he had created. "No, they're not here."

Uncle Jack straddled a bench and hung his head. "We'll find them, . . . but they'll have to be sent home."

Jordan looked up. "We've never sent anyone home—ever."

"We've never had campers who were a danger to themselves and other campers. What if others in your cabin had taken off with them?"

I heaved a sigh. Uncle Jack was right. "I'm sorry."

"Look," Jordan said. He threw his boot over the bench and stood.

"Ruben." I felt a rush of relief. Ruben, and on either side of him, Frank and Brad.

"Coming up short this morning, Professor?" Ruben said when Uncle Jack reached him.

"A bit." Uncle Jack met the trio midway between the pavilion and the library and rested a hand on each of the young campers.

Jordan and I sank back down on the bench, our backs to the table, elbows shoved behind us.

"Look at that," I murmured. "They're gone for hours, disrupt the whole camp, and all he does is pat 'em on the back."

Jordan let out a snort. "Not by a long shot. He'll spend half the rest of the day with them in the library, and then they'll be attached to him by invisible handcuffs. It's no picnic. I've been there." Jordan suddenly became solemn. "But he's sending them home."

"The Professor says we should have lunch," Frank said, wearing a smug expression.

I glared at him and then looked the other way. But immediately I berated myself. *The kid has problems. So, who doesn't?* I quickly thought, justifying myself.

Uncle Jack and Ruben stood some distance from the pavilion, talking and gesturing toward the canyon. Suddenly, Uncle Jack removed his hat, ran a hand comblike through his hair, and turned to look at Jordan and me.

"Uh-oh!" Jordan said. "I'm afraid Dad's finding out that Mary talked to María last Saturday. He'll know we asked Ruben to search for the meat thieves, and he won't like it at all."

I stared without speaking. Jordan was probably right.

"Not just meat thieves," Jordan said. "I think they're the ones who held up the convenience store and planted the gun."

My mind raced, wondering how Jordan came to that conclusion. I looked at him and then turned to watch Uncle Jack and Ruben. It didn't make sense.

Minutes later Ruben turned and strode back to the woods and Uncle Jack joined us at the pavilion. "Ruben is pretty sure the thieves are gone—have been gone for a couple of days. But we should be on the lookout, in case they return."

"We're not in trouble?" Jordan asked.

Uncle Jack shook his head. "Guess not. I'm just glad Ruben found the boys."

"Know what I think, Tony?" Jordan whispered a few minutes later. "I think Dad's glad we got María to call Ruben. Maybe even glad we didn't tell him, because if he knew he'd have had to tell the deputies."

"Speaking of deputies," I said, nodding toward the patrol car that was speeding toward the pavilion.

Uncle Jack called to Frank and Brad, "Wait for me in the library. I'll be over in a while."

Jordan glanced my way with an I-told-you-so expression.

Deputy Collins stepped from the patrol car. "More problems?"

"Yes . . . No . . ." I struggled to sound calm.

"Sorry about the call, Sam," Uncle Jack said. "Our missing campers turned up a few minutes ago."

Deputy Cole nodded. "We have business out here anyhow. We need to talk to one of your employees. A Henry Molenski."

So, I thought, *they're finally going to question Mole.*

Deputy Collins took out a small box the size of a notebook.

Fingerprint kit, I thought. *A humiliating ordeal.*

By early evening, Mary and I stood serving supper. Jordan poured juice and handed out cups.

"Oh good. Tacos."

"Two please."

"I'll take five." Tyler held out his tray.

"I have to leave," Frank said. His shoulders slumped, and the smug look was finally gone.

"Yeah, so I heard. Too bad," I said with no particular emotion.

"This is the most fun place I've ever been." Frank spoke softly and accepted his tacos quietly.

The most fun place you've ever been? My mind hung suspended between confusion and astonishment. *After nothing but complaints? The most fun place?* It didn't make sense.

"You just never know," Mary said after Frank walked away.

Frances joined us about the time the campers started returning empty trays to the kitchen. "You'll find this hard to believe," she said, almost in a whisper, "but Brad is staying because his parents and two little sisters can't be reached. They're on vacation."

"Vacation?"

"You're kidding!"

"Family vacation without Brad! Poor kid."

I was still awake at midnight, staring wide-eyed at the dark ceiling. Uncle Jack was taking David's place tonight, an arrangement that caused me more than a little guilt. It was really a simple duty, just keep twelve—no, eleven—boys safe for one night.

I wanted to be used by You, God, but I haven't been useful to anyone. If David had been here last night, probably Frank would still be here. Poor Frank. I remembered watching him sit at the pavilion—alone—his black hair mostly covering his eyes, waiting for his mother to come for him. I'd tried to think of something to say to cheer him up, but only Aunt Lisa's words kept filling my mind. "I'm so glad for your decision to make a commitment to Jesus tonight." But I couldn't say that to Frank. I couldn't think of anything to say to Frank.

And Quarto. The rodeo was getting closer every day, and we needed a lot more practice. The drills earlier in the day had been sloppy. Uncle Jack had been with Mole and the deputies and then with Frank and Brad in the library. I sighed and shifted to my side, restless and disappointed in myself and barely aware of the coyotes screaming far in the distance.

Tomorrow I'll spend the morning with Quarto, perfecting his pattern and working on speed. Tomorrow will be the start of serious training.

But tomorrow turned out to be a washout.

"Where have you been?" Jordan asked. "It was your turn to wash pots."

"Asleep . . . Okay? . . . Asleep!"

Jordan pressed on. "I let the screen door slam shut when I left for the shower shed this morning."

I shrugged.

"It's Frank, isn't it?" Mary said softly with a sad smile.

I shrugged again and heaped my tray with cold scrambled eggs and then poured myself a glass of milk. The campers had already come and gone and would be doing cabin activities for the rest of the morning.

Frances pulled her chair up to the end of the table and joined me with her cup of coffee. "You okay?"

"Sure." My head began to clear and my attitude improved.

Frances smiled in her grandmotherly way and put her hands firmly on the tabletop. "Time to work. Jordan, I'd like you to spend the morning at the library cleaning the windows on the inside. I've already put the buckets and rags there."

Jordan moaned and tossed his hat on a table before he strolled slowly in the direction of the library. I snickered.

"Say, Tony," Frances said, as she laid a hand on my shoulder, "you like pecan pie?"

"It's my all-time favorite."

"Good," Frances said, clapping her hands together. "You and Mary can shell these for me."

It was Mary's turn to snicker.

I looked to the spot where Frances pointed and my mouth dropped open. A fifty-pound bag of pecans. *She expects us to shell fifty pounds of pecans? No way.*

"All of them?"

Mary laughed, and Frances smiled. "Only enough for about ten pies."

What about Quarto? How will I ever make up for lost practice time?

Frances set two clean bowls and a large basket of pecans in front of us. Mary took a pecan cracker that looked something like a pair of pliers and squeezed it shut on a large nut, and then she took a sharp knife and pried out the meat of the nut.

I picked up two pecans, made a fist around them, and slammed the fist into my open palm. Crack! Both nuts broke into several pieces. I smiled and put the broken pieces in front of Mary and then reached for two more. We worked like a team.

"Guess you heard about Mole," Mary said, barely above a whisper.

"What about Mole?"

"Looks like he's the new suspect."

"Suspect? . . . You mean he planted the gun?"

"All I know is that the deputies told him not to leave the county. But that's funny, because Mole hasn't even left the camp in years, and I mean years."

"So how can he be a suspect?"

"Because he can't prove it. Sometimes we go days without seeing him, even though the horses are fed and the stable gets cleaned up."

"But . . . maybe he did it." Then I thought about Aunt Lisa's response to the idea. She sure didn't think so.

By lunchtime we had almost enough pecans for the ten pies. I knew they'd be good.

"I see Brad and his smiling face found another bold personality to shadow," I whispered when Jordan slid onto the bench ahead of me at camp meeting that evening.

"Yeah . . . a nice kid. Brad will be okay."

I leaned back, relaxing for the first time in hours, and picked up my Bible. I thumbed to the reference Dudley called out—glad again for the Sword drills I'd endured in Sunday school—and then I glanced over at Jordan.

"Great job on the windows," I whispered, nodding toward the obvious cloudy streaks across the glass.

Jordan smiled and shrugged.

Then I noticed his sunburned ears and an uncomfortable tension in my stomach made me reluctant to ask questions.

After more than half an hour Dudley invited the campers to make a commitment to Jesus and to let Him guide their lives and forgive their sins.

Without a second of hesitation, I was on my feet, following Brad to the altar.

"I'm real proud of you," I said, speaking right into Brad's ear. "You're making the right decision."

We talked quietly for several minutes as other campers and counselors kneeled down together near us.

"Let me show you some special verses from God's Word. We'll mark them in your Bible," I said, my heart pounding. "Look . . . right here in Romans 3:23 it says, 'For all have sinned, and come short of the glory of God.' "

"Even you?" Brad asked, sounding amazed.

"Even me. But look here in Romans 6:23. 'For the wages of sin is death; but the gift of God is eternal life through Jesus Christ our Lord.' "

Brad looked me full in the face, accepting, and waiting for more.

Encouraged, I went on. "The best part is that God made plans for this wonderful gift for us even while we were still doing bad things." I flipped back to Romans 5:8. " 'But God commendeth his love toward us, in that, while we were yet sinners, Christ died for us.' Pretty great, huh!"

More than an hour later, on my back staring up into the darkness, I was still thinking, *Pretty great!*

CHAPTER
12

"Well, you're certainly up and out early, young lady."

"Mornin', Professor. I heard you ride by on Colonel an hour ago," Mary said as she climbed the fence and sat on the top rail.

Uncle Jack smiled and nodded. He smoothed his moustache with two fingers. "Ever seen such a horse and rider?" Uncle Jack asked.

"A quarter horse, right?"

"Yep. They were bred to run the quarter mile faster than any other horse, and they're known for their quick burst of speed." Uncle Jack watched Quarto and me as we raced from barrel to barrel, circling each and then going on to the next. "I saw a quarter horse race a Cadillac for a quarter mile once. The horse won."

Uncle Jack stepped up on the fence rail, "Get your chin up, Tony . . . brace yourself with the saddle horn in the turn and let him feel you sit down hard . . . slow down in the turn . . . slow down. Too much 'go' and not enough 'whoa' in the turn can be dangerous. Good . . . good!"

Mary jumped to the ground and took several steps away when Quarto slowed and walked to the fence.

"Better, huh," I said.

"Much better," Uncle Jack said. "Frances will be waiting for you two. Better cool Quarto down and get on over to the kitchen."

I heard Frances humming before we rounded the corner of the pavilion.

"Biscuits smell good," I said, breathing deeply.

"Yeah," Jordan said, joining us.

"You're just in time. I'm waiting for the Professor to come sound the bullhorn. Five minutes till breakfast," Frances said.

"So where are my pecan pies?" I asked.

"I'll get started on them right after—" Frances stared at the top of the freezer. "Not funny, you guys. Where are the pecans?"

I stared blankly at Frances and then followed her gaze to the freezer.

"I left the shelled pecans right up there in a sealed gallon container," Frances said.

It began to dawn on me that the hours of work yesterday morning—hours that could have been spent working with Quarto—were for nothing.

"Why the pecans? Why not meat or vegetables?" I asked.

Frances removed biscuits from the oven and frowned. "Because everything else was locked up tight—the freezer, the cabinets, everything! There was just no room for the big plastic container."

"We need Judge Roy Bean out here," Jordan said as he put jelly on a biscuit.

"Who's Judge Roy Bean?" I asked.

"Just the best lawman west of the Pecos . . . about a hundred years ago."

Moments later Colonel came close to the kitchen and Uncle Jack dismounted. He looped the halter rope to a tree and then crouched down close to the ground.

"What is it, Dad?" Jordan called.

"Cigarette butt." Uncle Jack frowned and then listened as Jordan told him about the missing pecans.

"They're back."

Later, Mary and Jordan and I were quiet as we finished kitchen duty, but just beneath the surface was the silent buzzing of heavy thinking. *Ruben. We have to let Ruben know that the cave-dwelling-meat-and-pecan-thieves are back. What if they were also responsible for the convenience store robbery . . . and planting the gun? We had to reach Ruben.*

After lunch I sat on the bank of the river, my elbows resting on my knees, my fingers loosely laced together. I smiled as Dudley and more than a dozen campers waded out waist deep for the baptismal service. Amy and Rose huddled with several small girls, and Tyler and Aunt Lisa sat with a dozen or more boys, holding towels and smiling broadly.

Mary rested nearby on a large rock in the shade of a cottonwood. Her ever-present whistle hung from the leather cord around her neck, and her blue-rimmed sunglasses hid her green eyes. She reached down to pat Sabado. "Brad is glowing."

I nodded and tossed my hat to the grass. "I just wish Frank was out there too."

"I know," Mary said. She absently reached back and pulled her long braid over her shoulder and ran her fingers lightly up and down the plait. A bright yellow ribbon hung from the end of the braid. "The Professor says probably we planted the seed in his heart. In God's timing, someone else will see the harvest."

"Where's Jordan?"

Mary laughed. "Frances sent him back to wash the windows again. He did a terrible job yesterday."

Immediately I thought of Jordan's sunburned ears. *Something isn't right.* The words that kept coming to mind only sounded like an accusation. I'd keep the thought to myself for a while.

By early afternoon the buses had come and gone. Camp Jericho would be quiet again until the next busload on Monday morning. Sabado lay on the cool wood planks of the pavilion. Uncle Jack took out his journal and began to catch up on his entries as Tyler and Rose, the only counselors who did not go with the campers, started back to their cabins to prepare for a new week. I shook the ice in my cup and gestured to Jordan with my chin. *Ask him.*

Eventually Jordan cleared his throat. "Dad, María said she'd take us shopping in Acuna tomorrow, if you can drop us at Dudley's."

Jordan had said it casually, as if it really didn't matter, but a lot of thought had already gone into the plan.

You can almost see Uncle Jack putting two and two together, I thought. I looked away, lest my expression show too much eagerness.

"Dudley planning to be home tomorrow?" Uncle Jack asked.

We nodded.

"He'll be home studying all day, Professor," Mary said. "María can pick us up from there in the morning and get us back there by four."

Uncle Jack slowly nodded permission. I smiled.

It was the cloud of dust that caught our attention before we saw the Lincoln Town Car speeding toward the pavilion. Uncle Jack watched for a moment before his eyes showed recognition, and then he gently massaged his temples before he walked out to greet the visitors.

"Daniel Cleotelis." The gray-haired driver shoved a hand, heavy with jewelry, toward Uncle Jack. "I'm sure you remember me and my client, Michael Goodman."

Mr. Goodman wore a red-and-white striped silk tie knotted over a crisp white shirt. He had left his coat on the front seat of the air-conditioned car. "You made your position clear on our last visit, Mr. Vincent, but—"

"Nothing has changed, gentlemen," Uncle Jack said abruptly.

"Well, actually, it has, Mr. Vincent. You see, this property is adjacent to land that my company has invested thousands of dollars in, preparing to build a refinery. Do you know what a refinery could mean to Camp Jericho?"

I strained to hear, but I really didn't want to know.

Uncle Jack raised both hands and took a step back. "Whoa . . . I know exactly what a refinery would mean to Camp Jericho. Air that isn't fit to breathe, for one thing."

The two men glanced at each other. "Yes, well, the problem is that our stockholders insist that we have the extra thousand acres that comprise Camp Jericho. Without this property, the refinery will have to relocate."

Uncle Jack raised his eyes and creases lined his brow. "Start looking elsewhere," he said. "Camp Jericho is making plans for the final payment." I doubted that Uncle Jack felt the confidence he was showing.

"They just can't take Jericho," Mary whispered. Her eyes started to water.

"Well, I really would hate for you to lose your camp," Mr. Cleotelis said as he returned to his car.

That sounded fine, but no one believed it. "Nice meeting you too, pal," I murmured as the Town Car sped off toward the ruts and dips.

Uncle Jack returned to his bench under the pavilion and sat down heavily. "Training has to be a priority from now on. Forget kitchen duty, and pecans, and anything else that might distract you."

I nodded. "I'm sure Quarto can win this race." I spoke with a casual confidence that suddenly I did not feel.

Uncle Jack stood. "We'll leave for town tomorrow right after Quarto's workout. Concentrated training . . . starting first thing in the morning."

CHAPTER

13

Thunder rumbled, making the small cabin vibrate. Lightning lit the single room over and over, and torrential rain on the tin roof made me remember once standing too close to a fast moving freight train. Quarto wouldn't be saddled this morning.

I pulled the sheet up to my neck to ward off the dampness and then glanced down at the lower bunk just a few feet across the dark room. Mole had already left . . . if he had even come in last night.

With the first signs of dawn, the red minivan, its wiper blades whipping back and forth furiously, pulled up close to the cabin door.

Ten minutes later, Jordan and Uncle Jack and I entered the Vincents' back door and joined Aunt Lisa and Frances at the kitchen table. Aunt Lisa put a mug of steaming coffee in front of Uncle Jack. Rose came in from the living room, poured coffee for herself, and then pulled out a chair. It was a comfortable family gathering. I slouched back in my chair while Aunt Lisa poured hot cocoa in my mug.

Tyler's voice from the living room sounded over the rain on the roof. "I hope this isn't going to spoil your shopping trip this morning."

"Nah, the Professor says it'll let up soon," a softer voice answered.

Moments later, Mary stepped into the crowded kitchen.

Rain continued with less intensity when we climbed into the van, and light sprinkles peppered the windshield later as the van pulled up in front of Dudley's home.

Uncle Jack handed each of us an envelope. "Banks aren't open yet, but ask María to take you by to deposit most of this before you cross the border. It's cash."

First pay for a real job, I thought. *More than a hundred dollars.* I folded the envelope and slipped it into my back pocket.

"I'll be back around four o'clock."

We nodded and Uncle Jack drove away, splashing muddy water up on the sidewalk and leaving a wake to match that of a small boat.

"So," Dudley said, pulling out chairs from around the kitchen table and then shuffling his Bible and books and stacks of papers and pens into a pile, "going shopping today!"

"Umm." We nodded.

"Looking for anything special?"

"Well . . . actually . . . ," I said, not sure how much we should share with Dudley.

"Actually," Jordan said, "we're looking for Ruben."

"Ruben?"

Mary began at the beginning and filled Dudley in on all the details, from the stolen meat on the night I arrived, to the cigarette butt Uncle Jack found in the dirt yesterday. Dudley had heard most of the story already. The part about Ruben was news.

"Does the Professor know you're looking for Ruben?"

"Well . . . sort of . . . not exactly . . . no." Mary shook her head.

"I think maybe you should have talked to him about this." Dudley frowned and suddenly seemed uncomfortable.

At the border half an hour later, the weather seemed to change from rain to sunshine. María pulled her black Honda Prelude up to the immigration checkpoint. The border patrol guard leaned down and glanced in before casually waving us across the Rio Grande River.

"We don't need passports?" I asked.

"Not for one-day trips to Acuna. Hundreds of tourists and the residents around Del Rio cross every day. Shopping is good and prices are a lot lower on some things."

"So, where will we find Ruben?" I was impatient.

"My father tried to reach Ruben last night," María said. "They said he's selling horses at the market."

"The market?" I looked out the window as María pulled into a crowded parking lot only a block from the bridge.

"This is the shopping area. Lots of tourists. Lots of merchants. Ruben should be several blocks from here, but we'll walk through the malls to get there."

A small black-haired boy with a large, demanding voice stood in front of four other small boys—all barefoot and all dirty. "Wash you car twenty pesos?" He carried a pail of muddy water and a handful of wet rags.

María stood and pursed her lips for a moment; then her brows drew together, and she walked toward the boys with her fingers suddenly holding two dollars. She spoke rapid Spanish in a lecturing tone.

I watched, mesmerized by the sound of the language and María's sudden change of countenance. Her black hair hid her face when she leaned over with a finger jabbing toward the boys. She wasn't a lot taller than the tallest of the five ragged street urchins, but suddenly she seemed much more fierce. She never smiled.

"Sometimes it's best to pay them," she said, glancing back at her car several minutes later as we entered the mall.

The mall turned out to be not much more than an indoor flea market, its roof different from vendor to vendor, some sheet metal, some cardboard and plastic sheeting.

I kept close to María and fought to take everything in. Tourists wearing shorts and flowered shirts bought baskets and sombreros, and merchants followed prospective buyers down the mall offering a better price on passed-up goods.

A heavy, brown Mexican with a round face stepped in front of me, offering woven sandals several sizes too small. "You buy shoes? Forty pesos?"

" 'Fraid not."

"Thirty pesos?"

"Sorry." I moved forward slowly as the trader back-stepped in front of me.

"Handmade . . . excellent quality. Buy . . . you got a mama? Twenty pesos."

I hesitated and then pulled out my envelope full of cash. "How about ten?"

Suddenly I felt watched. My breath stopped a moment as I locked eyes with a tall, dark cowboy several yards away. It was the grin that made me most uncomfortable. The grin and the dark eyes fell under the shadow of a large sombrero. His faded plaid shirt was missing several buttons.

"C'mon," Jordan called.

I quickly nodded and shrugged my apologies to the vendor and then gladly escaped.

"Jalapeños," Mary said about the time my eyes began to water. She smiled and gestured to a table covered with open jars of peppers.

We examined baskets of mangos and papayas, fruit that I'd never seen and couldn't identify except for signs on the baskets.

Tourists—men, women, and children—and residents of Acuna crowded the mall, trading, buying, and selling. Adults, children, and dogs, even a chicken, wandered down the narrow, crowded corridor. Spanish and English surged through the air as shoppers dickered and bargained and finally pulled out wallets and purses.

"Ruben should be out this way," María said, stepping outside into an alley. "Paddocks are over there."

The air was fresher, and I took a deep breath. The muffled sounds of the mall were behind us, and the smell of horses and fresh hay began to get stronger.

"¿He veradas Ruben?" María said to a weathered old Mexican cowboy. His brown nose and wrinkled mouth was all that showed from under his wide-brimmed hat. His boots, creased black leather, could have belonged to his father and grandfather before him.

María listened, nodding, as the cowboy spoke Spanish so quickly that I couldn't separate the end of one word from the beginning of the next. The old cowboy gestured with a coil of rope and then shrugged before turning to walk away.

"He says Ruben is delivering horses to gold miners—prospectors—outside of town. He'll probably be there all day."

"Can't we go there?" Jordan asked.

María hesitated just long enough to encourage hope. "Well . . . maybe. Miguel says it's only about three miles down the road. Shouldn't be hard to find."

Frantic shouting suddenly had everyone's attention. "María! María!"

She hurried to an old black-and-rust pickup. The bed of the truck held crates of tomatoes piled higher than the top of the cab. The driver's voice rose and fell, high pitched and excited. His arms waved and gestured. María looked toward us as we waited on the sidewalk. She took several steps in our direction and then rushed back to the driver with more rapid-fire Spanish and waving of hands.

"What's wrong?" Jordan called.

"There's a small fire near my father's home," María said breathlessly, glancing back at the driver of the pickup. His arms were still waving. María's perfect English revealed only a trace of an accent. "You can get a taxi back to Dudley's house. I'm sorry. I'll try to talk to Ruben in a day or two."

"A taxi?" I said, suddenly feeling insecure.

"Stand right here. You'll be picked up within a couple of minutes."

Then she ran to the waiting pickup and raced off with the distraught driver.

Several moments passed in silence while we watched the pickup disappear down the narrow street. Cars, pickups, and buses passed in both directions. Acrid exhaust fumes hung suspended between the buildings and filled the narrow streets.

"Taxi," Mary said, and moved closer to the street. The cab pulled up, and the driver leaned over and shoved the back door open. Mary got in and scooted over. "C'mon," she called.

Jordan and I exchanged glances and hesitated.

"Come on," she said again.

"Well . . . ," Jordan said, "let's at least walk back through the mall first."

"No way." Mary's green eyes flashed.

"Just half an hour," I said. "We don't need María."

Reluctantly, Mary got out of the taxi, and seconds later it lurched away from the curb, the driver muttering words no one understood.

"Ever been here before?"

"Lots of times," Jordan said.

"Never alone." Mary shifted her small shoulder purse to the front of her and took a firm grip on it. "This is a really dumb idea."

Mary gestured to a street vendor. "Tamales, let's eat."

"Tamales?"

"Cornmeal and pork steamed in husks," Jordan said.

Other vendors, some with stands made from wooden crates, sold tortillas and tacos. The smell of a century of boiled frijoles and chili peppers filled the air.

We walked back through the alley toward the mall when a dark-skinned man suddenly stepped in front of us from behind a weather-beaten storage shed.

"¿Qué pasa?" I said, using half my Mexican vocabulary.

"I'll take the money." The stranger spoke perfect English and gripped a small handgun. His blue plaid shirt was missing several buttons, and his dark eyes were barely visible under the sombrero.

I recognized the grin. An evil, frightening grin. The same grin I'd seen earlier.

Within seconds the bandito and the three envelopes were gone.

Mary cried. "Our pay for two weeks' work just"—she flicked a hand—"vanished!"

"Deposit most of this in the bank," Uncle Jack had said.

God, a very present help in trouble? Yes, we were safe— unhurt, even in our disobedience.

An hour later Deputy Collins leaned against the side of his patrol car looking sympathetic when the Federales escorted us across the border. The red minivan straddled the white line, taking up two parking places and looking like it had pulled up in a hurry.

Long after the sun went down, the van pulled up near the door of the staff cabin, and Jordan and I climbed out. Uncle Jack cleared his throat. "Sheriff's office got another anonymous call Thursday. Caller says they're questioning the wrong guy concerning the convenience store holdup."

"Well, now what?" I asked.

"Ya' got me. I'll see the three of you at the library before daylight in the morning."

Jordan and I exchanged glances. "Right, Dad."

CHAPTER 14

Sabado barked. He barked and kept on barking until Uncle Jack finally ended the Sunday service—early. The little congregation filed out the double doors of the library and hurried down the wide path in the direction of the persistent noise.

"What is it?" Aunt Lisa called when we were fifty feet or so from the pavilion.

"Stay back," Uncle Jack said. An urgent tone edged his voice, and he hunkered down and called out to Sabado. "Come boy. He won't bother you. Come, Sabado."

The agitated barking continued with a fervor, and Sabado grew bolder and inched closer to the pavilion.

Uncle Jack raised his voice and took several steps forward. "Sabado, NO! Let him alone."

"What is it?" Aunt Lisa said again.

Everyone was straining to see, but Uncle Jack's caution held us back.

"Polecat."

Aunt Lisa let out a little gasp and took several steps back. "Oh no."

I suddenly stood up straight. "What's a polecat?"

"Skunk," Tyler said, also taking a step back. He began calling Sabado. Everyone called out to Sabado.

"Can't you just throw a stick or something and run the skunk off?" Rose asked.

"I wouldn't want to risk making a polecat mad. There's nothing—absolutely nothing—like the smell of a skunk," Uncle Jack said above the loud barking.

The smells coming from the kitchen at the moment were wonderful, I thought. Pot roast with potatoes, carrots, and onions simmered in a deep cast-iron pot. Frances had also cracked and sorted pecans and made two pies, and I was sure I could finish one off all by myself. I hadn't eaten since the tamales the day before. Uncle Jack's prayerful discipline had lasted a long time.

Sabado paced back and forth, staying about twenty feet from the kitchen where the small black-and-white animal, about the size of a barn cat, crouched down. Uncle Jack and the rest of us stayed a safe fifty feet away.

"Funny-looking skunk," Mary said. "No stripe down the back. He's sort of striped all over."

"Right," Uncle Jack said. "He's a spotted skunk. Not exactly spots, but that's what—"

Uncle Jack took a couple of steps closer. He lowered his voice. "Looks like the skunk isn't the only intruder in the kitchen."

Two men crouched next to the freezers, barely visible, cornered by the skunk. I recognized the red-and-white shirtsleeve I'd seen in the cave.

Suddenly, Sabado lunged forward, and we gasped and began to call out his name louder. The skunk lowered its head and began to hiss and growl. It stamped its right foot on the wood floor and then stamped the left. It raked the floor with long claws like a miniature bull and flipped its bushy tail.

Uncle Jack ran. Then everyone ran—except Sabado. Over my shoulder, I saw the skunk arch its back, and seconds after that the two-legged intruders ran from the kitchen, gasping and coughing. They disappeared into the woods.

An hour later the family of Camp Jericho shared bologna sandwiches at Uncle Jack and Aunt Lisa's home. The strong smell of ammonia, garlic, burning sulphur, and sewer gas all mixed together drifted over the camp.

Barrel racing practice began in earnest after lunch, and I was glad again to see that the ground had been dragged and the barrels repositioned. Mole remained a mystery. Quarto first walked the course and then trotted. Perfect practice was the goal, lest we reinforce bad habits.

Bad habits. Uncle Jack had talked about bad habits and the cost of disobedience since before first light. He had said that like bad habits, disobedience repeated became a pattern. Disobedience cost us two weeks' pay. It had inconvenienced and frightened many people, and we could easily have been hurt . . . or worse.

"Get his head up," Uncle Jack called. "Make him follow his nose and not his shoulder. Good . . . good . . . now smooch and cluck."

We trotted the course almost half an hour while Uncle Jack gave constant encouragement and support. Quarto's improvement was visible, and his attitude became more confident.

Quarto slowed to a walk, and then I dismounted. "He's doing good, isn't he!"

Uncle Jack nodded and reached for the reins. "Very good. He's ready to work at a canter now."

Uncle Jack tied two knots in the reins, about ten inches either side of center. "Use these as a guide," he said, and then paused and smoothed his moustache with two fingers. "I've got a young man coming this afternoon who can be a big help in your practice and training. He'll coach you and Quarto before breakfast every morning."

I frowned but kept quiet. Uncle Jack was a great coach. We were a team. I didn't need anyone else.

"His name is Bailey Jackson; he'll take David's place. David's parents picked him up from the hospital yesterday. He's doing fine, but he won't be coming back."

"Aren't we doing okay without this Bailey guy?"

"We are, but Bailey knows barrel racing. He has the trophies to prove it."

I began practice at a canter—a slow gallop—but my heart wasn't in it. *What if Bailey, this guy with all the trophies, wanted to take over, enter the contest himself. Would Uncle Jack allow it? What about all the hours of practice we had already put in?* It didn't seem fair.

"Okay . . . lean in . . . grip the horn . . . slide your right hand over to the knot. Good . . . that's better. Now drive your feet deep into the stirrups and line him up for the second barrel. Great . . . you got it . . . good . . . good!"

Sunday night beef stew was replaced with hamburgers grilled over a pit dug in the ground overlooking the river.

"I sure miss those pies," Tyler said, staring out across the canyon.

"Weren't fit to eat," Frances said. "Had to toss the pot roast too. And I'll just bet those two guys hiding in the woods tonight don't smell so good."

Aunt Lisa stood and brushed the dirt from her hands and then used her hat to slap dust from her jeans. "There he is."

Uncle Jack got up from the ground and headed out to meet the newcomer.

My fears of being replaced vanished. Bailey stood at the far side of the field of bluebonnets, his cane supporting a stiff leg, and a wide belt supporting his extra-large girth.

"Does it always smell so bad around here?" Bailey said, his eyes watering.

Laughter echoed across the canyon.

"And that dog you got tied to the tree is worse." Bailey took his handkerchief and covered his nose.

For the first time, the skunk incident seemed funny, but only for a moment.

"Wash him in tomato juice," Bailey said with an air of superiority.

"We did."

"What about lemon juice and vinegar?"

"Tried that too."

"Buttermilk?"

"We've tried everything," Mary said, "even baking soda and dish soap. Only time will get rid of that smell."

"Well, I won't be able to sleep without fresh air," Bailey said, as if he were the only one enduring the foul odor.

Jordan and I exchanged glances.

Just before dark Uncle Jack stood and stretched. "Got a few things to do. Ready, Lisa?" Uncle Jack held out his hand and helped Aunt Lisa up. "Jordan, how about taking Bailey to David's cabin . . . and after breakfast in the morning you can show him around before the campers get here."

Bailey, his cane poking at the ground, slowly followed Jordan across the field.

Frances and Rose collected the remains of supper—drink cans, paper plates, and trash—and then headed for the kitchen.

"We'll be there in a few minutes," I called to Frances and then looked at Mary, causing her to sink back to the ground.

"What?" she said.

I looked at the receding figures of Jordan and Bailey in the growing dimness and lowered my voice. "Remember what the deputy said last night about another anonymous phone call made last Thursday?"

"Yeah . . . ," Mary said. "So?"

"So . . . Thursday was the day Jordan did such a poor job on the windows in the library . . . remember? And he left his hat at the pavilion . . . and Thursday night I saw his ears. They were sunburned. And . . . if he made the phone calls, then he was probably the one who planted the—"

"Stop it right there." Mary jumped up from the ground, brushed dirt from her jeans, and then raised her chin and spoke slowly, pronouncing every word with emphasis. "Jordan is your cousin. How can you even think of suggesting such a thing?" Mary wheeled away and hurried to join Frances and Rose.

Quarto stood saddled and waiting when I arrived at the stable at dawn Monday. A faint flush of anger swept over me. That wasn't like Mole. He should know that saddling and bridling a horse was an important time of bonding between horse and rider. I checked the girth straps and began talking softly to Quarto.

"Well, it's about time you got here," Bailey said, as he stepped from the tack room. His tone held a subtle hint of humor, but he smiled in a condescending way that made me more than a little irritated.

"So . . . you've done some barrel racing," I said, trying to sound casual.

"Five years ago, when I was your age."

"Won a few trophies?"

"Sure did, and this was the last one." Bailey waved his cane in the air. "Kicked by a stallion."

Black curls twisted out from under Bailey's hat, making his pale, round face look too large for his short stature.

I removed and replaced the bit in Quarto's mouth and then led him to the paddock.

"Walk him through the pattern for a while," Bailey called.

I began at a trot, knocking over the first barrel and reaching the second at a canter. I gripped the saddle horn and leaned down to upright the barrel and then continued the pattern at a trot and later at a canter for most of an hour.

Bailey kept up a steady stream of negative instructions. "Slow down . . . you're out of step . . . he's not bending . . . no . . . no . . . no." Bailey shouted orders and waved his cane in the air until I began to find it easy to ignore him altogether. *This will not work out.*

"Hey Bailey," Mary said, as she climbed the fence and sat on the top rung. "How are they doing?"

Bailey shook his head sadly and pinched his lips tightly together as if it were just too terrible to talk about. I galloped to the stable and dismounted in a leap. *He'll never win.* I'd heard it . . . even though Bailey hadn't said it. It was written all over his face, but who was he anyway? Probably hadn't ridden a horse in forever and was a terrible coach. Surely Uncle Jack would agree.

Uncle Jack did not agree. "He's come all the way from Fort Worth. Give him a chance. I can see that you two are clashing spurs, but he's willing to try again if you are."

"What? You mean that guy's been complaining to you about the way I ride?"

"He has more experience with the rodeo than I have, and he can help you if you'll let him."

Uncle Jack took off his hat and looked toward the sky before he spoke. "God promised to be a present help in time of trouble. Jericho is in trouble."

I thought of my own troubles.

"God sends help in different ways. I believe God has a purpose for Bailey at this camp."

Uncle Jack spoke his piece and then turned and left.

"P-u-e-e-e!" María cried as she and Amy stepped off the bus with their campers a few hours later. "What's that awful smell?"

"This isn't bad at all," Mary said. "You should have been here yesterday."

Seventy-two campers, most holding their noses and complaining loudly, left the two buses and slowly found their way to the counselors they had been assigned to. They unloaded bags and pillows and various pieces of sports equipment, and then the buses made a wide circle in the clearing and headed back to town.

"A few more French fries," I said, holding out my tray an hour later.

Jordan frowned and tossed a couple more fries on my pile. "You can't practice all the time. We could use some help in the kitchen."

"Sorry." I shrugged with a helpless gesture and then smiled. "You heard what Uncle Jack said."

Frances tapped a wooden spoon on the bottom of a large pan. "I heard what he said, but I know what he meant. I think you'll have plenty of time to wash pots before the afternoon trail rides start."

"Yes, ma'am."

Mary and Jordan bowed to each other in good-humored mocking.

Moments later, when Jordan set his tray next to mine, Bailey waved his cane as he herded his group of campers from the pavilion.

I watched several moments, holding my third hamburger suspended in the air.

"Well?" Jordan said.

"Well, what?"

"I said, what do you think about our new counselor?"

I shrugged. "I don't think anything about him."

I put my half-eaten hamburger down, carried my tray to the kitchen, and walked toward the stable.

"Hey," Jordan called. "You gotta wash pots."

The day passed with a flurry of activity. Trail rides, swimming, volleyball, cabin activities, and competitions. I sat in the back of the library that evening and let my mind absorb the sights and sounds. Energetic campers filled the benches, most laughing and talking with counselors and new friends. Voices rose and fell, none distinguishable from the others. I saw sunburned necks everywhere. Dudley and Tyler stood talking near the handmade pulpit while Uncle Jack and Aunt Lisa sat on the front row, partly turned around and talking to campers on the row behind them. Mary, her golden braid and blue ribbon lying across the front of her shoulder, played the piano and looked out over the assembled campers. Bailey reached forward two rows and tapped a camper on the shoulder with his long cane. The small boy lowered his shrill voice and continued talking. A warm breeze seemed to hurry through the large, open windows. I crossed my arms loosely and leaned against the back of the bench.

Soon Uncle Jack quieted the group and for the next fifteen minutes gave the usual greetings to new campers. He explained the rules, answered questions, and introduced the staff. Then, after twenty minutes of fast-paced spiritual choruses, and after Aunt Lisa's familiar Monday evening song, Dudley opened his Bible and began to read.

" 'Be ye therefore perfect, even as your Father which is in heaven is perfect.' Matthew 5:48." Dudley paused and looked out over the seventy-two campers and the staff. "Anyone here perfect?"

Heads shook side to side, and campers glanced around as if making sure they were not the exception.

"None of us are perfect, are we? Not you. Not me." Shoulders seemed to relax and eager heads nodded. "But Jesus in your heart is perfect." Dudley allowed a long pause before he went on to explain what God had provided for us.

My mind began to drift, and I remembered Uncle Jack's caution. "Perfect practice makes perfect." Not that Quarto and I would ever be perfect in the race, but reinforcing mistakes by repeating them would lead to failure. He had said almost the same thing Sunday morning before dawn when he had said that allowing mistakes, failures, and sin to go unconfessed and unrepented only lead to more of the same and to spiritual death.

Dudley spoke loudly and with enthusiasm while my mind sang. *On Christ the solid rock I stand, all other ground is sinking sand, all other ground is sinking sand.*

CHAPTER

15

Quarto moved from a canter to a gallop at first light Tuesday morning. We'd practiced almost half an hour before I saw Bailey lumbering across the ground, his cane poking holes in the dirt.

"Jordan was late," Bailey called.

Jordan had been asleep when I slipped quietly from the cabin forty-five minutes earlier. Bailey couldn't leave his campers until Jordan arrived to supervise their morning activities. I smiled and then focused my concentration on the next barrel.

Bailey launched a monologue of negative commands. "Don't look at the barrel. You're holding out the wrong side of the reins. No . . . no . . . you got his head too low."

Bailey took a timer from his pocket and waited several moments before he hit the start button. He watched intently as Quarto raced from barrel to barrel, circling each one and then straightening before racing to the next.

He pressed the stop button and then shook his head slowly with a frown. "No way."

I guided Quarto to the fence. "How fast?"

"Twenty-one seconds."

"That doesn't sound so bad."

"Last year's winning time was 16.675 seconds."

"Oh."

"Try it again. Don't hold him back."

"Right." As if I'd been deliberately holding him back.

Quarto ran the pattern at a gallop several more times before breakfast, never getting faster than eighteen seconds. Bailey's frown deepened, and his shoulders sagged. He shook his head as if thinking how much better he could have done.

The bullhorn sounded. Five minutes till breakfast. I led Quarto to the stable and began the half-hour of cooldown and cleanup when Mole appeared, almost from the shadows, and reached for the reins.

I hesitated only a moment. "Thanks, Mr. Molenski." I patted the horse with rough affection. "See you before lunch, Quarto."

"Who was that guy?" Bailey asked after we'd left the stable.

"Just a friend who works here."

I saw the green seconds before Bailey did and caught myself before I reacted.

"Got it," Bailey called, bending on his good leg to grab the ten-dollar bill. The money disappeared through the bushes as his fingers brushed it.

Young boys laughed, and then we heard the sound of feet scampering away. Bailey's face flushed red. "Kids," he said, as though it could have been anyone else.

"Hey, Sabado." I leaned over and stroked the golden retriever. "You still don't smell so great, . . . but you're better than you were."

"How'd you do?" Mary asked.

"Eighteen seconds."

"Great."

"Not great at all. But I'm working on it."

Bailey relieved Jordan and joined his group of campers as they stood waiting in the breakfast line.

By the time Mary and Jordan and I carried breakfast trays to a table, most of the campers were on their way back to their cabins for morning activities.

I thought of our earlier walk to breakfast. "Ol' Bailey almost got himself a little richer this morning."

Mary smiled. "Seems like someone in every group tries that one. He asked me if I had any nail polish remover."

I laughed out loud at the thought of Bailey with red toenails.

Three hours later—long enough to allow Quarto to rest—I was back in the saddle circling the yellow-and-orange barrels at a fast gallop. After fifteen minutes of good practice, correcting mistakes and working on consistency, I heard Uncle Jack call out.

"Use your inside rein and leg going into the turn . . . good . . . that's right. Now use your outside rein and leg coming out of the turn. That's it . . . talk to him . . . okay . . . good. Give him his head between barrels. Rate down for the pocket . . . good . . . good."

"Rate down for a pocket?" Mary asked, as she climbed the fence and sat on the top rung.

"Hey, Mary. Means slow him down when he starts to circle the barrel or he'll shoot right past it."

After almost half an hour more of hard work, I dismounted. Mary jumped to the ground and moved away from the horse.

"Looks like you two are doing great," Mary said, staying a safe distance from Quarto.

I looked from Mary to Quarto. "It's okay. He won't hurt you."

Mary only shook her head and hurried off toward the pavilion.

"It took years just to get her near the stable," Uncle Jack said. He was thoughtful for a few moments, stroking his moustache, before he changed the subject. "With a work-out before breakfast and again before lunch, I think Quarto should skip the trail rides. Don't want to push him too much."

I glanced at the stable but said nothing.

"Why don't you ride Colonel in the afternoons." Uncle Jack nodded, as if confirming his decision, and turned and walked toward the pavilion.

A big smile spread across my face. "Thanks," I called out. "Thanks, Uncle Jack." *Ride Colonel. Great. It was as if Uncle Jack had said, "Here, go drive my Cadillac."*

During the next three weeks, I practiced barrel racing before breakfast with Bailey's supervision—except on mornings when Jordan failed to wake up in time to stay with his boys. Before lunch we drilled for another hour, usually with Uncle Jack's encouragement. Quarto's time improved but fluctuated between sixteen and seventeen seconds. I rode Colonel in the afternoons.

On a Thursday—early evening—Mary hung the last pot on a hook over the sink. "All done."

"I've washed enough trays and pots and pans to last a lifetime," I said.

Mary smiled. "Me too."

"You going back to the cabin before camp meeting?" Jordan asked.

"Yeah, need a quick shower and clean clothes."

"How about bringing my Bible and a pen when you come?"

"Right. See you in the library."

I cleaned up, put on a fresh shirt, and left the cabin, letting the screen door slam shut. "Jordan's Bible," I said out loud and then went back inside, allowing the screen to slam shut again. I opened the top drawer of the dresser, picked up the Bible, and began to rummage under Jordan's jeans and shirts for a pen. I picked up a silver pen and shut the drawer when I suddenly realized that it wasn't a pen at all. It was the size and shape of a pen, but it was definitely no pen. I stood for several moments, my mind sorting a tangle of thoughts and my heart rate picking up speed. "Oh no." I'd have to keep this revelation to myself for a while and think about it . . . pray about it, too. My heart became very heavy.

"Thanks," Jordan said, taking his Bible. "No pen?"

I shrugged and slid into the back pew behind Bailey. "Couldn't find one."

Friday afternoon was quiet at Camp Jericho. The buses had come and gone, Jordan was helping his mom with a mountain of laundry, and other staff members who hadn't left with the campers were busy at their cabins. I sat absently staring across the canyon. My shoulders sagged, and my chest heaved deep sighs.

"So, what am I supposed to do now, Lord?" I said softly. I snapped a flower from its root and absent-mindedly picked its bluish-purple petals, letting them fall to the dirt between my boots. Low clouds, white and puffy, drifted above the canyon and the jagged hills in the distance. *Peaceful, quiet clouds,* I thought. Very unlike the turmoil that raged within me.

I took off my hat and slung back my damp waves. "What should I do about it?" I murmured again.

"There you go again," Mary said, startling me from my brooding. "Talking to yourself." She sat down on the ground near a small patch of bluebonnets.

I grimaced, silent several minutes until Mary moved to stand. I cleared my throat. "Wait. Maybe you should see this."

I reached in my shirt pocket and took out the wrinkled newspaper clipping that the deputy had given Uncle Jack weeks earlier. I handed it to her and then looked away, as if distancing myself from something unpleasant.

Mary read the article aloud, glancing my way several times with a questioning expression.

Late Wednesday evening, two men held up the Handy Foods Convenience store on Highway 27 outside San Angelo. The pair held a clerk at gunpoint and kept him blinded for several minutes with what appeared to be a silver laser light pointer attached to a leather cord. They left with an undetermined amount of cash. Sheriff's deputies immediately put out an all-points bulletin for the arrest of the men.

Mary finished reading. "So?"

"So . . . I found this in Jordan's drawer last night." I handed her the silver penlike object hanging from the leather cord. "It's a laser pointer."

Mary's fingers trembled as she took the pointer, and I could tell by the look in her eyes that now she believed me. Jordan had put the gun in my bag. But why?

Tears glistened in her eyes as she spoke. "What now?"

"I don't know. I just don't know."

"Maybe you should talk to the Professor and Aunt Lisa."

"Maybe . . . but think how broken up they'll be. Jordan's really a good kid. I think—I hope—he'll do the right thing on his own. Let's just give him a little more time."

Saturday evening I sat under the pavilion with Mary and Jordan and the few staff members who were still in camp. Bailey had been invited to Dudley's home for the weekend. Rose and Amy were with María.

"Oh, I almost forgot," Uncle Jack said. He reached into his shirt pocket and then handed me a letter. "Looks like it's from your mom."

I opened the envelope and read silently. A small smile spread larger and larger until I felt like it included my entire face. "Listen to this," I said, and then began to read a few lines. "I'm so pleased to hear about your commitment to Jesus. It makes me remember the wonderful change in your father after he became a Christian. I look forward to hearing more—a lot more—when you get home. Maybe I'm ready for a new life too." I folded the letter and stuffed it into my back pocket, hoping no one had noticed the catch in my voice.

I leaned back against the table and thought a moment about the depth of happiness I felt just then. But within seconds, the satisfied feeling left and a nagging worry began to creep in again. Uncle Jack and Aunt Lisa would be hurt deeply when they learned of the trouble Jordan was in. There was no doubt that they would eventually know. I wouldn't make it to Greenwood with this hanging over my head, and Jordan needed to clear his conscience—voluntarily or otherwise.

Uncle Jack leaned forward and rubbed his moustache with two fingers. "Deadline is coming up on entry fees to the rodeo. Qualifying events start in three weeks."

Aunt Lisa rattled the ice in her cup. "How much is the entry fee?"

"Hundred dollars."

She kept an expressionless face, but I imagined her thinking how many magazine articles she'd have to write to earn that much money. Or how Uncle Jack would have to cut corners on camp expenses to get it. Then I remembered the envelopes of cash that Jordan and Mary and I had lost because of careless disobedience in Mexico. Yes, one hundred dollars would be a sacrifice for Camp Jericho. Quarto and I had practiced morning and afternoon today and would drill again Sunday afternoon. By gate time at the rodeo, we would be ready.

A new group of campers spilled off the buses at noon Monday, and another week of activities began. It was a routine that I looked forward to now. Predictable, and yet exciting.

By late morning Tuesday, Quarto was running the course for the second time. Uncle Jack called out reminders and support. "Put most of your weight in the stirrups . . . good . . . now drop your weight back in the saddle. Drop your outside hand to the saddle horn . . . now . . . good. Very good. Don't you feel the difference when—"

Uncle Jack stopped midsentence when a Val Verde County patrol car pulled up to the stable.

My chest tightened, and my hands formed tight fists. Not now. I wasn't in any mood for a confrontation now. I slid to the ground and led Quarto around to the front of the stable for water and a cooldown.

Deputy Cole got out of his car and looked around, unsmiling. He adjusted the belt that held his gun holster and then removed and replaced his dark glasses. It occurred to me that the deputy might be nervous. Probably only my imagination. *Do deputies get nervous?*

Before he spoke, Jordan and Mary appeared, out of breath, from the narrow trail that led to the pavilion. I locked eyes with Mary for a quick moment and avoided eye contact with Jordan. *What now,* I thought. *Will I be arrested?*

"Professor." Deputy Cole acknowledged Uncle Jack's presence and then looked toward the stable. He took a pair of handcuffs from his pocket. "No one can give your hired man, Mr. Molenski, a solid alibi, and he does have that old arrest record. I've come to take him in for questioning."

I heard a faint gasp behind me and fought to keep from turning. It had to be Jordan.

Uncle Jack moved closer to the deputy. "No, I don't think so."

"Get Mr. Molenski," Deputy Cole said. His voice was harder, and his eyes began to narrow. He was clearly on a mission and felt that he had finally found his man.

"Look," Uncle Jack said, his voice rising and his frustration beginning to show. "Henry Molenski is no more involved in this matter than . . . than . . . than I am."

Before the deputy could respond, Mole appeared from the tack room. He stood near the door and shuffled several steps toward Uncle Jack. He removed his dirty hat, his fingerprints visible all around its brim. The sun reflected off his shiny head, and his shoulders sagged.

I could hear little crusty sounds coming from Jordan's throat. *Come on, Jordan, do the right thing.*

Deputy Cole walked toward Mole with a determined pace. "Hands behind your back."

"No!" Jordan finally screamed. "It was me." Then he sank to the dirt on his knees and cried aloud with great sobs.

Uncle Jack stood frozen in place for several seconds, lips parted and eyes darting from Jordan to Mole. Everyone's boots seemed attached to the ground. No one spoke for three or four seconds. Only the sound of Jordan's anguish filled the air.

Suddenly Uncle Jack was on his knees with his arms wrapped tightly around Jordan's trembling shoulders.

An hour later Deputy Cole left Camp Jericho—alone—and only Mary was still teary.

Jordan had confessed again his jealousy over my position at the camp and his fear that Uncle Jack might feel more love and respect for his nephew than for his son.

"I found the gun and the laser light in a cave the afternoon before you came," Jordan had said. "I hid the gun in your bag the next morning—a quick way to have you sent home."

Then, as Uncle Jack said, "Like sin often does, it grew and became a monster."

"I wanted to confess a thousand times," Jordan had said. "I saw right away that I'd like Tony, and I hated what I'd done. But . . . it was too late." Jordan had tearfully begged my forgiveness and received it.

Uncle Jack walked with Jordan to the staff cabin to collect his things. He'd move back to the house with his mom and dad for the rest of the summer.

I watched them go and felt a sharp pang of compassion for Jordan and then love and admiration for his dad. Jordan was lucky. No, Jordan was blessed.

I took a deep breath and stared at a white cloud. As if chains had been dropped from my chest, I could finally breathe again. The way was suddenly clear. This rodeo win would be more impressive on my record than even the summer at Camp Jericho. I smiled.

CHAPTER
16

The faint call of the bullhorn Wednesday morning was weak and ineffective, barely audible at the paddock. Bailey and I left the stable and walked to the pavilion.

"Where's Uncle Jack?"

Frances frowned. "Blow this thing for me, will you honey."

I pressed the end of the horn firmly to my lips, took a deep breath, and blew hard. My face must have turned purple.

"Thanks. That should bring 'em."

"Where's Uncle Jack?"

"Oh . . . just out riding."

"Now? He's always here to meet his campers for breakfast."

Frances hesitated, as if trying to form her words and then stepped to the grill to turn strips of bacon.

"Is something wrong?" I was beginning to feel some concern.

Frances took a deep breath. "He spotted smoke from a campfire up the canyon last night. He's taken off on that horse of his to find those men. Took his rifle. Your Aunt Lisa's worried. So am I."

"He wants to get this over with for Jordan, doesn't he?"

"I guess so."

Mary and I stood behind the serving line as campers offered trays to be filled.

"How's Jordan?"

"It'll take a while. He feels terrible about what he did to you."

I nodded. "You know where Uncle Jack is?"

Mary frowned and then nodded. "He took his gun."

"I know. I'm going to help him."

Mary gasped. "No, you can't. Those men are dangerous."

"I know. I spent a day with them, remember?"

"They didn't know you were in the cave then. You can't go out there."

"I have to. And don't say anything to Frances . . . or anyone else."

A short time later I tied Quarto to an Ashe juniper near Colonel and then walked along the edge of the canyon. Devil's River forty feet below looked clear and shimmering in the morning sun. Uncle Jack was not in sight.

Cactus and sage crowded the trail. I walked almost a mile along the gorge and searched the steep walls below. The wind made a faint singing sound as it circulated through the canyon, and an occasional bird—mourning dove or grackle—stirred the air as it moved from tree to tree. I stopped suddenly and smiled as I counted the white-tailed deer.

Then I sank to my knees, staring down through the dense brush and mesquite growing along the canyon wall. All at once my attention was snagged. A boat rocked gently in the water. *Their boat,* I thought. I watched for more than half an hour, moving only my eyes as I searched the canyon for Uncle Jack.

About the time my knees began to cramp, I was struck in the face with the sharp glint of the sun on shiny metal. I flinched and then worked to focus my eyes through the brush below. Uncle Jack. He sat cradling his rifle, crouched in a clump of sage not twenty feet below. *How long had he been there? He sees the boat, and he's waiting for the robbers to come for it,* I thought. I picked up a chunk of limestone about the size of a pencil eraser and tossed it toward Uncle Jack. He didn't notice. I tried again, and Uncle Jack turned his head slightly. A deep frown settled over his face. You shouldn't be here, it silently shouted.

Uncle Jack gestured with a palm out stop motion, and I shrank back almost out of sight and waited. I waited more than an hour, yawning occasionally and relaxing against an outcropping of limestone. I scratched my mosquito bites. Maybe this was a dumb idea. Uncle Jack didn't need me after all, and it was near lunchtime by now.

"Hold it right there," Uncle Jack shouted, startling me from my thoughts. I moved quickly on hands and knees to the edge of the embankment and looked down. Uncle Jack had his rifle aimed toward the river, and two men, mostly hidden behind brush and rocks, clambered toward the small boat. Seconds before the men reached the water's edge, I heard a deafening rifle blast that echoed through the canyon many times before it faded. Water gushed up through a hole in the bottom of the boat, and the two men turned and hurried back toward the safety of a cave.

"Tony," Uncle Jack shouted. "Go call the sheriff. Ride as far as you have to for good reception."

I took off toward Quarto, jumping cactus and occasion- ally stumbling on gravelly patches of limestone. I ran with all my strength the mile to where the horses were tied and then mounted Quarto with an adrenaline rush of energy.

Within minutes I reached the carport. "Aunt Lisa," I shouted breathlessly, "I need the cell phone. Quick."

Jordan appeared at the door. "What's wrong?"

"Gimme the phone. Uncle Jack has two men cornered in a cave. I've gotta get the deputies."

Aunt Lisa hurried past Jordan and handed me the phone, and I took off in a gallop up the trail behind the house.

I rode half a mile before I stopped and tried to make the call. Only static buzzed through the earpiece. A mile further I tried again, and again heard static.

Please God, just let Uncle Jack be okay. Further up the hill, cactus and brush became more dense, and the trail became less and less distinguishable. I rode almost another mile, picking my way around hedgehog cactus and Spanish daggers, before I pressed the 0 again. An operator came on the line, and then immediately the connection was broken. *Getting closer to reception,* I thought.

In the distance, almost half a mile, stood one lone cottonwood tree. By far the tallest tree in sight. I tied Quarto to a sycamore and took off on foot, stepping around crippling cactus and praying out loud as I went. Travel on foot was now faster than Quarto had been able to move over the past half mile.

I reached the tree and looked up through its high branches. Getting up to the first branch would take some real effort. The ground below was covered with the dried remains of catkins, heavy clusters of greenish flowers. Their cottony seeds formed a spongy layer of earth below the tree's branches. I moved out from the trunk of the tree and jumped to grab hold of the lowest of the spreading branches. By pulling the branch down as I moved back toward the tree, I was able to get a firm grip on a larger part of the branch and then hike myself up. After that, climbing up higher was as easy as going up a ladder.

"Deputy Cole," I said. The reception was not bad. "This is Tony Vincent. My uncle is holding two men in a cave at gunpoint about a mile up the canyon from Camp Jericho."

The conversation was brief. I put the phone back into my pocket and made my way back down the ladder of branches.

I lowered myself from the last branch and hung suspended several feet from the ground and then let go. My right boot fell flat, but under the sole of the left I felt something alive, heaving and rolling. I watched in horror as the body of a large rattlesnake, sulphur yellow with deep pits on each side of its head, began to move away. Brown diamond-shaped spots dotted the body.

In a flash of lightning panic and almost convulsed movement, I jumped away from the snake, violently twisting my right knee. Then I fell to the soft spongy layer of catkin-covered ground. All the work and hours of practice with Quarto—useless in a flicker of time.

Two weeks later I stood looking out over the paddock. "Drive your feet into the stirrups . . . toes up, heels down . . . loosen up and take a deep seat . . . spread your hands evenly on each side of his neck . . . good . . . good . . . good." I leaned on my cane, a support that I'd need for several weeks, and coached as Jordan raced around the barrels. A few days of dependence on that cane had given me a whole new view of Bailey and his obnoxious stick.

"Better, huh?" Jordan said, a few minutes later.

"Much better." So much had happened during the past couple of weeks. The two guys Uncle Jack cornered? In jail for a long, long time.

The last group of campers had left along with Bailey and most of the other staff. It had been a happy, but tearful, good-bye. With the rodeo only days away and a knee that would take months to heal completely, I had gladly agreed to help coach Jordan for the barrel race. I took Bailey's stopwatch from my pocket. "Try it again."

Twice a day Jordan and Quarto practiced, perfecting the pattern and increasing speed. I offered support and encouragement.

"Does he stand a chance?" Mary asked. She climbed the fence and sat on the top rail.

I nodded. "He's doing great. Got him down to seventeen seconds most of the time. Sixteen, on really good days."

Mary sighed. "But now you won't have a rodeo win to help you get that scholarship for the horse training school."

Greenwood. I had thought about that . . . more than once. "Well . . . maybe I can report that I helped coach a winner."

I looked away, struggling with my thoughts. "You know, being with Uncle Jack this summer has been kind of like having Dad back. It'll be really hard to let him go—again."

Mary nodded and said nothing for several moments before she spoke. "Years ago the Professor gave me a special verse from the Bible. He said it was just for me." She smiled. "I used to think it was only for me. It's from Psalm 68:5 and it says that God is 'a father of the fatherless.' "

I turned my attention back to the paddock. "Spread your hands and find the knots in the reins," I called out. "Drop your outside hand to the saddle horn . . . good . . . good. Now pull up on the horn and get in stride with Quarto. Right . . . you got it. Real smooth."

Quarto galloped through the pattern another half-hour, and then Jordan brought him to the fence. "Well . . . ?"

"Sixteen seconds is your best time. But those automatic timers at the rodeo measure to the one hundredth of a second."

Jordan flashed a confident smile. "We'll keep practicing."

"Only perfect practice makes perfect," I said, remembering Uncle Jack's caution. "Don't ever reinforce mistakes or imperfections by repeating them." I knew that Uncle Jack hadn't been talking only about barrel practice.

Friday evening Ruben drove into Camp Jericho, pulling a horse trailer. Uncle Jack and Jordan stood talking with him near the stable. I watched from a distance, deliberately allowing Jordan time and space with his dad.

"A father of the fatherless." A special verse. I felt as if it were only for me.

I sat with Frances at a table under the pavilion an hour later when I caught a glimpse of Ruben. He rode Colonel, heading out of camp.

"Big day tomorrow," Frances said.

"Sure you don't want to come?"

"I've seen my share of rodeos."

"This one is special."

"It sure is, and I'll be praying that Jordan will do his best."

I rubbed my stiff leg. "No more coaching. He'll be on his own."

Frances smiled. "Well, not exactly on his own."

CHAPTER

17

It was still dark Saturday morning when Frances set hot biscuits and a plate of sausage and eggs on the table. Fluorescent tubes lit the pavilion, and excitement and anticipation seemed to electrify the air.

"Quarto ready?" Aunt Lisa asked.

"Loaded and waiting," Uncle Jack said. He helped himself to another biscuit.

"So, how long a drive is it?" I asked.

Uncle Jack set his coffee mug on the table. "Should take us about three hours. We'll be there before the qualifying events begin."

Aunt Lisa drove the minivan. I sat in the back with my stiff leg stretched out, and I focused on Mary's long braid hanging over the back of the seat. Her blue ribbon almost touched my knee. Uncle Jack and Jordan followed the van in Ruben's pickup. It took almost forty-five minutes to ease the truck and trailer over and through the deep ruts in the dirt and gravel drive to the highway.

Then, within half an hour we were on Highway 90 and passing the small town of Fort Clark Springs. Fields of cotton bordered the highway, and patches of bluebonnets covered the median between eastbound and westbound traffic. Acres of tomatoes grew on the north side of the highway, and then we passed fields of honeydew melons and maize.

"Corn?" I asked, gesturing out the window to the south.

"Looks like corn, but it's sorghum," Mary said.

Cattle—Santa Gertrudis and Black Angus—covered the hills in the miles before and after the town of Uvalde. Oil wells dotted the land where the cattle grazed.

We passed exit ramps for Knippa and Sabinal, and other small towns.

"Smell that?" Aunt Lisa asked.

I wrinkled my nose a moment. "Onions."

"Right. This area is known for its onions. In fact, the famous Vidalia onions from Georgia were originally developed here." She said this as if I had a profound interest in onions and their history.

San Antonio. Ten miles. The van, followed by the pickup and trailer, left Highway 90 and soon we were in sight of the rodeo grounds. Pickups and horse trailers seemed to be parked everywhere. Vans, travel trailers, and campers sat next to picnic tables, folding lawn chairs, and coolers. Dogs roamed freely, and little kids played in the dirt.

Aunt Lisa parked under the shade of an ebony, its branches almost scraping the roof of the van. I poked the uneven ground with my cane, searching for firm support. Cowboys with lariats practiced roping fence posts. Little boys sat on bales of hay, pretending to ride bulls, and the smell of popcorn and cotton candy filled the air. It was a carnival atmosphere.

Uncle Jack caught up with us before we reached the arena. "Jordan is checking in. Elimination events start in about an hour."

"You mean Quarto could be out before the competition ever starts?" Mary asked, sounding worried.

Uncle Jack shook his head. "He'll make it. He just has to run in under nineteen seconds."

Jordan joined the family after the trial runs. His score, 17.487 seconds, ensured his place in the competition. Uncle Jack had told Jordan not to push Quarto too much. Most of the riders scored in the seventeens or eighteens. None pressed their horses to run like they would in the final competition. Of fourteen entries, only one failed to qualify.

At noon the rodeo began with the Grand Entry. Contestants, members of the rodeo committee, saddle clubs, clowns, and local officials paraded around the arena. The national flag was presented, and the national anthem was sung.

Then six poles, placed twenty feet apart, were set in the center of the arena, and the first event was started. Pole bending. A timed event where participants had to weave in and out around the poles. More than a dozen contestants took turns racing around the poles, each timed with an electronic beam of light. Dust filled the air, and crowds of spectators cheered. "Quarto could do that easy," I said.

The second event, bareback bronc riding, started almost immediately after the poles had been cleared from the arena. "Rules here are simple," I said to Mary. "Just got to stay on that horse for eight seconds. The rider can hang on with only one hand, and his free hand can't touch the horse anywhere." A bronco shot out of the chute, his rider hanging by one hand to a strap wrapped around the horse just behind its withers. His free hand whipped the air.

"Doesn't look simple to me," Mary said.

Almost two hours later Jordan and Uncle Jack stood, ready to leave the bleachers after the steer wrestling and calf roping events. "Time to get Quarto warmed up," Uncle Jack said.

A heaviness settled over me. I sighed and my shoulders slumped. The thought crossed my mind that maybe God's plan for me didn't include Greenwood. I tried to dismiss the idea.

Aunt Lisa reached over and patted me on the back. "Go on down to the warm-up pens and watch."

I shook my head, "Naw . . . this is Jordan's time." *And maybe it really should be Jordan's time,* I thought. Jordan had worked hard and was as fast as I had been. And besides, if Jordan won, it would look pretty good on the Greenwood application to show that I had coached the winner. Wasn't that what Greenwood was all about—learning to teach? I straightened and forced a smile.

"Look at the clown," Mary said.

I followed her gaze. "Yeah, but they're not just out there to be funny. They're the bull rider's best friend. They can distract an angry bull long enough for the rider to scramble to safety. Even the bronc riders are glad for the clowns . . . except when they're heckling them for getting thrown."

The loudspeaker popped and crackled. Next event. Barrel racing. During a fifteen-minute intermission, the arena was dragged smooth and a fine spray of water settled the dust. Then three barrels—each one a bright red, white, and blue— were set in a triangle pattern in the arena.

I gestured to the ground. "Let's hope Quarto is one of the first called; otherwise he'll be eating the other horses' dust and stumbling in their tracks."

Horses of all breeds—Morgans, Appaloosas, and quarter horses—prepared to enter the race. Bright colored saddle blankets—royal blue on pale gray Appaloosas—added to the festive atmosphere.

The scratchy public-address system echoed across the arena. "First up, from Abilene, Texas . . . Rosa Rodriguez riding Señorita Raya."

I shifted forward and gripped my cane in both hands. I resisted the urge to stand while Señorita Raya pranced nervously in the alleyway, preparing to bolt into action. At Rosa's invisible signal, the horse suddenly vaulted forward and then crossed the electronic beam of light at a full gallop. The clock was set in motion. Rosa circled the first barrel with a smooth, tight turn and lined up for the second. I glanced at the clock, a large electronic timer mounted just below the second-story judges' booth. Five seconds. Señorita Raya circled the second barrel, leaning in enough that it looked like Rosa could have reached down and scooped up dirt with her inside hand. She returned both hands to the reins and lined up for the third barrel. Dust filled the air and crowds of spectators gasped, some standing to their feet, as Senorita Raya rounded the third barrel, bumping it slightly. The barrel rocked back and forth for an uncertain moment and then settled back in place. No penalty. Rosa crossed the beam of light, stopping the clock at 16.457 seconds. Good time.

I sat back and took a breath—my first since the clock was set in motion. "No problem," I said, smiling at Mary. "Quarto can beat that." *I hope!*

Next up, Carmen Mendoza, from Harlingen, Texas, riding Caballo Atriso. Carmen struggled with her horse, reminding me of stories I'd heard of horses that were alley-sour, overly agitated by long periods of waiting to be called. Caballo Atriso pranced, almost uncontrolled, before he took off in an uncertain gait, breaking into a full gallop only after the clock was set in motion. An almost perfect ride had been spoiled by a bad start. Carmen's time was 17.675 seconds.

The next rider, Hank Johnson, a teenager about my age, crossed the beam of light and circled the first barrel in under five seconds. I rose from my seat only a few inches before my stiff leg brought me back down. "Get his shoulder up . . . get his shoulder up," I murmured. The horse, Nevada, rounded the second barrel, shouldering in and left the barrel rolling across the dirt. Five-second penalty. Then a final score of 22.012.

After one more rider, a tall black-haired cowboy from Waco, the winning time still stood at 16.457 seconds, scored by Rosa Rodriguez on the first run.

A horn sounded and a tractor pulled onto the field. "Good," Mary said. "If Quarto's called next, he'll have smooth ground."

I nodded and again fought the disappointment of sitting in the bleachers rather than entering the race. I took a deep breath, pasted a smile across my face, and kept quiet.

After almost fifteen minutes, the next horse and rider were announced. And then the next and then the next. Each horse and rider scored close to, but never under, the winning 16.457 second time. Rosa's remained the winning score when the tractor once again pulled into the arena to grade and smooth the ground.

"Next up, from Del Rio, Texas . . . Jordan Vincent, riding Quarto." The sound vibrated through the air, and my heart pounded. I gripped my cane and leaned forward intently. Mary and Aunt Lisa held hands and also leaned forward, as if for a better view. Quarto appeared in the alleyway, excited, prancing more than I would have expected, and surging with energy.

My chest swelled with pride as Jordan spread his hands on either side of the saddle horn and firmly gripped the reins at the knots Uncle Jack had tied.

I spoke softly. "Drive your feet into the stirrups . . . toes up, heels down . . . loosen up and take a deep seat . . ."

Then, at some unseen signal, Quarto seemed to explode into the alleyway, setting the clock into action and stirring a cyclone of dust up from the smooth ground.

"Keep your hands low . . . good . . . good." My voice was lost in the excitement of many hundreds of voices. Quarto made a tight circle around the first barrel, and I remembered the hours he had spent at a slow trot, learning to bend and flex as he rounded the barrels. Jordan then lined him up and galloped straight to the second barrel. The turn there was almost too tight, leaving the barrel wobbling but still standing.

I gulped for breath. A five-second penalty if the barrel had tipped would have been as good as a disqualification. "Rate him down . . . rate him. Good. . . . Now one hand on the horn. You got it. . . . Give him his head."

I coached and Jordan performed as if he had heard every word. Jordan's time, 16.145, made him the current winner.

Aunt Lisa and Mary hugged and smiled and hugged again.

This win, with me as coach, almost assured me of the position at Greenwood Equestrian High School. Dad would have been proud.

Only four riders to go. "We haven't won yet," Aunt Lisa cautioned, holding her hands out, palms down, in a let's-calm-down gesture.

"I know, I know." I did know, but I knew with my head and not with my heart. Twenty minutes later, a harsh and disappointing reality settled on all of us. The last rider was a seasoned cowboy from Dallas. His time, 15.890 seconds, won the cheers of hundreds. Cameras flashed as the judges handed him a check for twenty-five hundred dollars. Friends and family congratulated him. The cowboy smiled broadly.

"No," Mary whispered, and then leaned her face down to her open palms.

"So close," Aunt Lisa said. Her voice sounded hoarse.

The crush of disappointment made my chest hurt. I stared at my boots. *What now, God?*

It was a subdued group that sat at the pavilion the next afternoon. I stroked Sabado and absently stared into the distance, thinking of Oklahoma City and home. In a few hours I'd be on my way. An unusual peace settled over me—not a happy, joyful kind of peace, but a comfortable resignation. Greenwood. Things would be all right. I smiled and a deep well of contentment rushed over me. Mom wanted to hear about my new life and the commitment I'd made to Jesus. I could hardly wait to tell her.

A cloud of dust rose above the small trees to the south, and then we spotted the Val Verde County patrol car. Then, as if in hot pursuit, the patrol car raced past the pavilion before coming to a stop halfway to the library. Uncle Jack glanced at Aunt Lisa and shrugged before swinging his boot over the bench and walking to the waiting officer. Deputy Cole got out and leaned against the hood of the car, his arms crossed in front of him.

I found it a challenge to keep my spiritual contentment. Jordan frowned and we exchanged glances. We watched Uncle Jack smooth his moustache with two fingers and then use one finger to push the brim of his hat up a couple of inches. Conversation rose and fell, but distinctive words melted in the breeze.

"Look," Frances whispered. Deputy Cole handed Uncle Jack an envelope. Aunt Lisa and Mary stiffened and leaned forward, straining to catch words. After what seemed like a long conversation, the deputy got in his car and circled back toward the entrance to Camp Jericho. Uncle Jack stood motionless until the car was out of sight.

Suddenly I jumped from the bench and raced stiff-legged toward Uncle Jack. "What is it?"

"What is it, Professor?" Mary said, catching up.

"Dad? Everything okay?"

Frances and Aunt Lisa followed. "What is it?"

Uncle Jack smiled and his eyes glistened. "God has provided a way for Camp Jericho to continue." He removed a check from the envelope. "There was a reward for the capture of those two men. Seems that they were wanted for robberies all over the state."

"Look at the amount," Aunt Lisa said, wiping away tears. "Exactly five thousand dollars."

A little past midnight, over six hours behind schedule, the bus left the outskirts of Del Rio. All of Texas seemed dark and quiet.

I settled back in my seat and let the now-familiar verse drift through my mind: *God is our refuge and strength, a very present help in trouble.*

I smiled.